Total-E-Bound Publishing books from KS Augustin:

On Bliss
Prime Suspect
A Pirate's Passion

His Bodyguard

GUARDING HIS
BODY

KS AUGUSTIN

Guarding His Body
ISBN # 978-1-907280-72-6
©Copyright KS Augustin 2009
Cover Art by Lyn Taylor ©Copyright 2009
Interior text design by Claire Siemaszkiewicz
Total-E-Bound Publishing

His Bodyguard

GUARDING HIS BODY

Dedication

To my good friend Maria Zannini, for suggesting
the idea in the first place. It's all her fault!

Chapter One

"Was anyone hurt?"

Yves de Saint Nerin looked across the glossy expanse of his mahogany desk to his personal assistant. His expression grim.

"Non," Guy Aubrac replied.

Yves' blue eyes glittered. "Small mercies."

He swivelled in his chair and looked out the glass wall that separated his study from the cold air outside. Below him, the street lights of Grenoble twinkled serenely, snaking through the small city like festive decorations, while almost all of the buildings' lights remained dark. And why not? It was two o'clock in the morning after all.

He should be back asleep, Yves thought, not sitting here brooding and impotently planning revenge. Upstairs, his warm and rumpled bed beckoned, the only spot of relaxation in a day that had suddenly turned chaotic with the potential of a meltdown in his Amsterdam office. That was why he was still here in Grenoble, instead of Lyons where he had promised to be. He had averted disaster in the Netherlands only to court it back in France.

"Where are they now?" he asked of the glass, confident that Guy was still standing nearby. The young man had been his assistant for two years and was well used to how he ran his business and his life. Although, he conceded blackly, this urgent, early morning wake-up call was a bit unusual even for him.

"Your sister and family have moved to her husband's chateau in Verneuil."

Yves grunted. That was something else he was not entirely happy with. Surely Adrienne knew she could have come to him — after all, he was her elder brother. But instead, she and her twin babies had no doubt acceded to her husband's wishes and sped their way to Theron's extensive estate in the Champagne region.

This was yet something else for his brother-in-law to hold over his head. As if it wasn't bad enough that he had already been accused of being aloof, boorish, and notably absent from his sister's upbringing since the death of their parents, now Theron was going to accuse him of putting his sister and children at risk. Yves steepled his fingers and gazed out into the darkness. The problem was Theron was right.

He was due to spend the weekend with Adrienne and her toddler twins down in Lyons. But the emergency at Amsterdam had sprung up. Then this. He would get everything sorted out as quickly as possible then spend the weekend with Adrienne and the children, trying desperately to make amends. All under the cynical eye of her husband, Theron Dauzat, no doubt. Just the thought of it made Yves grit his teeth.

"What do the police say about the fire?"

"The accident investigation team is still on site," Guy replied, his tone apologetic. "I'm sure they won't come to any initial findings until later this morning."

"It was arson," Yves bit out. "The scoundrels know they can't get me here, so they try for where they think I will be. Someplace a little less secure."

"Oui, monsieur. That sounds, most probable."

Yves spun the chair until he was once again facing the timber-faced warmth of his inner sanctuary. His icy blue gaze bored into the hazel depths of his assistant's.

"It was Alexandrov, wasn't it?"

Guy shrugged, a typically Gallic gesture, and opened his hands wide. "Monsieur, we can't know for sure until–"

"It was Alexandrov, wasn't it?" Yves interrupted, repeating his question more insistently this time.

The younger man admitted defeat with a tired nod of his head. "So it would seem."

"And now, not content with accepting defeat on its own merits, he seeks to sway me by attacking my family."

"As you say, monsieur."

"And who will be next?" Yves wondered bleakly, more to himself than Guy. "Now that he has failed again, what other innocent will he target? Will he go after Theron's vineyards, or the villages that surround them? My businesses in Paris and Grenoble? The charities I support? How can anyone remain safe while Alexandrov roams free?"

"If I may, monsieur, I doubt Leonid Alexandrov will go after your other interests. I believe this is personal."

Yves frowned. "What makes you think so?"

"He only targeted your sister's house in Lyons at a time when you were supposed to be there. If he was interested in hurting your interests or those close to you, he could have attacked Madame Dauzat's at any time since you refused him your assistance, two months ago."

Two months ago, when he thought he'd seen the last of that cunning businessman. He had been sure to have their final meeting in the heart of Paris, where there were lots of witnesses around, in case Leonid Alexandrov tried anything. But, even though the stocky Russian was angry, Yves thought the man had managed to control his obvious disappointment. After all, as he had told the other man at the time, a businessman couldn't win every battle. Even he had lost deals in the past. Dealing with the loss had been a way of making himself stronger. Obviously, Alexandrov was not of that same opinion.

He hadn't heard from the Russian in two months and thought the man must have moved onto other, greener pastures. He should have known better. Alexandrov didn't like to lose. Well, Yves didn't either.

"So you're saying he's after me, in particular?"

"It would seem so."

Still, where did that leave him? Was he always going to have to look over his shoulder, wondering if the Russian would target him while he visited his family? Or his latest mistress? Was this all part of a bigger plan, to deprive Yves of his quality of life—his business, his family and female companionship?

Yves tapped his fingers impatiently on the smooth lacquered wood of his desk, while his gaze swept his study. This was his inner sanctum, where only Guy and the cleaning staff were allowed entrance. Tall, handcrafted timber shelves reached almost to the ceiling, crammed with books. In one corner, a large freestanding globe rested, looking magnificent in its carved oak frame. Persian rugs dotted the floor, bringing muted jewel colours to the room.

Ten years ago, when he bought the hillside property on the rocky slopes near La Bastille, the entire building could have almost fitted into the study. It was a humble hut with a magnificent view. And it was also extremely difficult to get to. The workmen and materials for Yves' magnificent hideaway had to be brought in by helicopter, and they had toiled away for two years, building his vision of what a home should be.

Besides his study, the main building also contained the formal and living areas. Two wings sprouted on either side of the house, enclosing a courtyard with an elaborately hedged garden in front of a heated swimming pool. One of the wings belonged to Yves, the other was for his sister's visits.

The house should have been pale and ornate, dominating the rocks next to the notorious La Bastille and the city of Grenoble, but Yves left such ostentations for other men. He made sure the stone used to construct his house came from the local region, so his home blended into the slopes of the mountain. With the exception of the lights that sometimes blazed from the windows, and the occasional helicopter that thumped overhead, the

11

inhabitants of that French plateau could live their lives in complete ignorance of the wealthy man who lived on the treacherous incline above them.

Leonid Alexandrov knew he couldn't strike at Yves while he stayed in Grenoble, or when he was surrounded by his security phalanx in Paris, so he had waited until opportunity presented itself, via Yves' only sister, Adrienne, and the weekend he was scheduled to spend with them.

Yves eyes darkened as he remembered the past two hours — two of the longest he had ever lived through. The fire had sped through his sister's house in Lyons in minutes, it seemed, but the smoke detector system had done its duty, and Theron, Adrienne and the twins had rushed to safety, while their home burnt to ashes.

Theron Dauzat had no doubt on whose shoulders blame fell, and it had been a little past midnight when the chirping of Yves' mobile phone woke him from sleep. Only a handful of people knew his private number, and Yves had snapped to full wakefulness in a second, flinging the sheets to one side and picking up his phone. He'd pressed the talk button and heard Theron's angry voice blasting down the line at him.

Yves didn't even try to defend himself as his brother-in-law had vented every ounce of resentment and frustration at him.

"I don't care who you are, Yves, but the spill-over from your life must stop," Theron had finally told him, after stopping to draw a much-needed breath.

Yves had sat on the edge of the bed and let the other man give voice to his fears. Usually, nobody — man or woman—dared talk to him like that. But this was family, and family always had that right.

"Isn't it enough that you neglected your sister for years-"

No, that had been too much, and Yves had been stung into a reply.

"Adrienne had the best education in Switzerland," he'd shot back. "She was safe and secure, and she wanted for nothing."

"Nothing, except for some affection from her rich brother. Besides the car, and the clothes and the jewellery, what else did you give Adrienne, Yves? Tell me."

"I will not have this argument with you again, Theron," Yves had answered grimly. "Have you called the police?"

Theron's laugh had been slightly hysterical. "Rest assured that the fire-fighters and the police arrived long before I decided to make this call."

"That's good. I'm glad that Adrienne and the children are safe."

"You're not slipping off the hook that easily. If your sister isn't confronted by salacious rumours of your mistresses—a different one each month—then she's at the mercy of your unsuccessful business dealings. You may think your glib words of sympathy for my family mean something, but I know you better than you think."

That, too, was an old jibe, made worse by the fact that Theron Dauzat, indeed, knew how men like Yves thought...because, until he'd married Adrienne, he had been one of those men himself. During the months of their courtship, it had been Yves who had repeatedly warned his sister to be cautious. He'd sent Guy on numerous errands to dig up the worst information on Theron so he could present his sister with inconvertible proof of the man's unsuitability to be within a few feet of her, much less conversing, and dining—and other things—with her. Had Adrienne listened? No, of course she hadn't, and Yves had grimly prepared himself for the worst. But, much to his surprise, Theron had proposed marriage and now, five years later, they seemed a very contented couple with two energetic sons. Yves still couldn't believe how he had miscalculated that situation, much as he was doing now.

He had fully expected to hear from Theron that they were headed to Grenoble, and he'd even thought of putting his brother-in-law on hold while he made the necessary transport arrangements, but it looked like—once more—Adrienne had outmanoeuvred him, heading for her husband's extensive estate in Champagne rather than coming to him. It had hurt to be presented with his sister's obvious preference and that, too, had been the reason he'd allowed Theron to bluster. It was his fault. Much as he hated to admit it, his sister really was safer with her husband than she was with him.

The call had ended on an unsatisfactory note, but that hadn't stopped Yves. Dressing quickly in a pair of loose pants and a casual linen shirt, he'd used the intercom to call Guy, who lived in a small self-contained chalet next to the main house when they were at Grenoble. Within half an hour—before the clock struck one o'clock—both men were in the study, reviewing what had happened.

Despite Theron's assurances, Yves hadn't rested until he had the head of the Lyons police department on the phone and had listened to what was being done while his sister's house still smouldered. Part of him had wanted to rush to the city, even though there was nothing more he could do. The blaze was already a few hours old, Theron had removed his family to Champagne and the emergency services seemed to have everything well in hand. But Yves still hadn't been satisfied and was about to call for a helicopter, when Guy had suggested that was perhaps what Leonid Alexandrov would have wanted.

"If he failed to get you in the fire, perhaps he has some thugs waiting for you, in case you decide to visit the scene in person."

And so here he was at two o'clock in the morning, wide awake and staring morosely around his exquisitely decorated study while his sister headed for safety away from him.

"The chief of police knows my suspicions," Yves told his assistant.

"They can't do anything until the accident investigation team confirms the cause as arson," Guy remarked.

"And in the meantime, Alexandrov is free to roam around and make my life a misery." Yves' drumming fingers turned into a fist that hit the desk's surface. "Am I to remain hermetically sealed until this man is put behind bars?"

"That would be the safest," Guy murmured, then grimaced as he saw the thunderous expression on his employer's face. "Although not very practical."

"Wherever I go, I will continue to be targeted, until this matter is taken care of." He pushed back his chair with impatience and got to his feet, pacing the length of the study in his bare feet. "I could stay and conduct business from here in Grenoble, but that would be like admitting defeat. On the other hand, any visit to a friend or a charity event, has the potential for disaster. Damn him! He has me just where he wants me."

Guy said nothing.

"But I refuse to give in." He strode over to the tall glass wall. It was still so early that dawn hadn't touched the horizon yet. "I will not remain cooped up," he told the darkness, "but neither will I be where he expects me to be."

Yves didn't have to look at his assistant to hear the puzzlement in his voice. "I don't think I understand."

"At the moment, I've been spending most of my time in France, but I have business interests elsewhere, do I not?"

"Oui."

Yves' voice strengthened as he warmed to his theme. "Of course, going to Russia would be asking for trouble, but there are other destinations besides Europe."

"America, you mean?"

Yves walked over to the world globe, flicking it nonchalantly with a lean finger. "America." The sphere twirled silently. Asia.

His eyes narrowed as he stopped the spinning, gazing at the spot right under his fingers. "Didn't we get a proposal from an overseas software company? Tech-88 or something similar?"

"Yes, we did."

"Where are we at with that deal?"

"As per your instructions, I sent the proposal packet to our departments to vet."

"And...?"

"They appear to be everything they say they are. Their business case is sound, their financials are solid, but they lack capital for expansion."

"While I have the capital but no foothold yet in that region."

"I was going to go over all those proposals with you next week, monsieur."

"Perhaps that's not going to be necessary, Guy," Yves remarked, still looking at where his hand rested. "Where did you say Tech-88 was based?"

"Er, Australie. One of the northern cities, I think."

Yves smiled at the globe, and at the blue of the Great Barrier Reef, right next to his hand.

"Guy, there are some travel arrangements I'd like you to make."

* * * *

Helen knew she stank. She must. She let out a breath and got to her feet, reaching for the towel that was beside her workout mat. Her legs ached, but it was a delicious feeling, satisfaction from the cool-down at the end of a strenuous session she had just completed. She wiped runnels of perspiration from her face with the towel and headed for the large open window.

The sounds of traffic — cars mixed with trucks — assailed her ears from three floors down. Even though she was tucked in a side-street, Fortitude Valley in Brisbane was always bustling, a large arterial road cutting straight through it from the northern to southern suburbs, across the busy Story Bridge, carrying vehicles at every hour of the day and night. She had found it comforting being lulled to sleep by the sounds of movement, and waking up to it. It reminded her that she was alive and there were still things she needed to do.

Alive. Her hand stilled as she rubbed her hair, the tendrils dark with perspiration and curly at the ends. But as much as she loved living in the centre of a thriving metropolis, reality had a way of cropping up when she least expected it. Just as it had three months ago.

No, she wouldn't think about that. Not now.

Helen grimaced and turned away. Brisbane had been a home to her for all of her twenty-six years. And, until a few months ago, it had treated her well. Her gaze roamed the expanse of her loft apartment, where walls existed only to enclose a goods elevator, two bathrooms, a kitchen, and suggest a minimal attempt at privacy. The large mullioned windows let the sub-tropical sun stream through and caught the rich texture of the polished pine floors, looking warm and comforting against the brilliant white of the tall walls and high ceiling.

The whole floor was hers — the top storey of an old warehouse right in the middle of Brisbane's liveliest inner city suburb. By the time she bought the apartment shell, the idea of warehouse living had taken off in the city, but buyers were still reluctant to purchase a residential property in one of its most notorious locations. Helen, on the other hand, had seen the location's potential more as an opportunity and had signed a contract on the place as fast as she could pull a pen into her hand. Now, in the late afternoon, a pleasant breeze blew through the open windows, airing the large space completely and lifting the gauzy white curtains so they resembled birds' wings fluttering in the wind. It was October, and the chill of winter had well and truly disappeared, bringing with it a balmy warmth and the promise of more heat to come.

At the thought of another humid summer, Helen started perspiring again. She turned and was about to head for the bathroom when her phone rang. Normally, she let the answering machine take it, but she was close enough to the low, teak coffee table to reach down and pick up the receiver herself.

"Hel," she said succinctly, using her nickname. Now that she stood still, she thought she could detect the aroma of sweat and exertion on her body. She sniffed experimentally at her underarm and wrinkled her nose. It was lucky for everybody concerned that nobody shared the apartment with her.

"Hel, it's Ryan." The welcoming voice of Helen's sometime employer filled her ears, and a smile instinctively curved her lips.

"Hello Ryan. What can I do for you? Do you have another workshop you want me involved in?"

"Ask not what you can do for me," he replied with a laugh. "Ask what I can do for you."

"Really? Like what?"

"Nothing I can really discuss over the phone. Would you care to meet me for a coffee? I can be in the Valley in about twenty minutes."

"That sounds perfect. How about I meet you at Carlo's?"

"Carlo's it is. See you then." And he clicked off.

Helen replaced the receiver thoughtfully and continued her walk to her bedroom, a roughly rectangular section of floor that was partitioned off with carved timber screens. Behind them, closets lined part of one wall, ending at a corner, behind a large futon bed.

She had been expecting a call from Ryan — they hadn't spoken for almost a week now — but she hadn't been expecting anything more from him, especially when she already knew his workshop and training schedule. He certainly had her intrigued.

Helen entered her bathroom, expertly flipping the damp towel into the laundry basket, and following it up in quick order with her shorts, T-shirt and underwear. Even though the bathroom was enclosed with walls, light still illuminated the space, thanks to a skylight she had installed when she first began refurbishing the warehouse floor. The other bathroom was the same — walls of small white tiles, separated by lines of iridescent blue glass squares, with the skylight illuminating everything from above.

She showered under the cool water, letting the massaging streams carry away the sticky sweat and tiredness from her body. When she was done, she towelled herself dry with a marine-toned bathsheet and padded to the bedroom to look for something to wear.

Ten minutes later, she traipsed down the small flight of steps at the front of the building and walked up the street to Brunswick Mall, less than a five-minute stroll away. Her hair, unruly at the best of times, was kept back from her face with a dark, stretchy barrette. She thought it was a simple and easy solution, unaware of how the accessory showed off the delicate angles of her cheekbones and emphasised her large, candid, blue-grey eyes. Her denim capri pants only partially covered lithe, muscular calves, and the scooped neck T-shirt outlined a feminine figure that could easily be swamped in more bulky clothing.

She walked happily down the mall, unaware of several covert and appreciative masculine gazes, her long limbs swinging freely and her bearing confident.

Fortitude Valley had always been a haven for immigrants to Brisbane, starting with the Scottish in the mid-1800s. Since that time, other communities also started businesses there—Italians, Chinese—and it was now a dynamic and cosmopolitan part of the city's life. Carlo's was one such example of a migrant's small cafe that had morphed into a landmark for the suburb. It was named after the current owner's father, who had worked the small coffee shop for more than twenty-five years, before passing it on to the next generation. Vinnie, Carlo's son and a shrewd businessman in his own right, had extended the premises, creating a separate dining area for the evening restaurant goers, but also not forgotten the cafe's original customers. Small round tables and wicker chairs jostled for space in the paved area outside, and it was here that Helen settled herself, after calling out her usual order to the smiling wait staff. Vinnie, a cheerful man with a smile as wide as his head, waved to her before moving to the large, chrome coffee machine that dominated the area behind the long counter, to prepare her order.

It was a nice time of the day, late afternoon before the workers in the city finished for the day, and Helen watched the grandmothers trundle along with their wheeled trolleys full of groceries. It was a time to relax, with the heat from the sun gone, and just its light left, slanting across the buildings, and throwing the elaborate sills and decorations of the mall's historic facade into myriad lines of light and shadow.

Later on, the children and shoppers would disappear, and the Valley would be home to a different population completely—couples looking for a restaurant or bistro, and people looking to enjoy themselves at one of several bars that dotted the area. If only they restrained themselves to just enjoying themselves, she thought bleakly, and shivered despite the warmth. The partygoers wouldn't leave the district until the early morning, and then the Valley would settle down to one or two hours' peace, before the bakers arrived, heading for their shops, and the cycle would begin all over again.

She didn't want to think about that. Not about dark nights, and not about what happened that had turned her entire life upside down, but her memory was relentless. She remembered Pete, tall but a little too skinny to pass for a bouncer at one of the city's nightspots. She remembered how he'd smilingly agreed to help out a friend. And she remembered–

"I see you got here before me." Ryan's gruff voice boomed close to her, and she looked up at him with startled eyes. She hadn't even seen him coming. At the same time, their coffees arrived—a latte with no sugar

22

for Helen and a long black with two sugars for Ryan Greenwood. Vinnie had obviously spotted him long before Helen had.

She smiled and waved him to a chair to her left. "Sorry, Ryan, I must have been miles away."

"That's what bothers me," he muttered as he sat down.

Ryan was a quintessential Queenslander, from his tall and broad build to the freckles that dusted his skin. His hair was a sun-bleached brown mixed with emerging grey, and his eyes were blue. The tip of his nose always looked like it was on the verge of sunburn, a redder hue than the rest of his ruddy complexion, and his hands were broad and meaty. Creases radiated outwards from the edges of his eyes, matching the frown on his forehead—a permanent reminder of decades of squinting into a bright and unforgiving sun. He was a man who had seen and done things most people only imagined, and Helen considered him her best friend.

"And what's that supposed to mean?" she asked, although she knew very well what he was getting at.

He harrumphed and turned his attention to the coffee, stirring it carefully with a spoon and popping the sliver of accompanying biscotti into his mouth, dry.

"You know you're supposed to dunk it first, don't you?" Helen asked with patient amusement.

"I like it like that," he replied, crunching through the nuts and hardened pastry. He drank deeply from his cup and, when he put it back on its saucer, half of the coffee was already gone. "So how are you bearing up?"

Helen shrugged and dropped her eyes, taking a more demure sip of her latte. "Okay."

"That's a pile of bullshit." He paused. "Pete is gone, Hel. I know you were close, but he's not coming back."

"You know," she said, still looking at her glass, the coffee within it the colour of pale milk chocolate. "I think I'd come to grips with it better if it hadn't been such a senseless death."

Peter Dodd had been a good friend and fellow martial artist. He worked for Ryan as an instructor at his martial arts academy, much as Helen herself had done before she branched out into her own business. In such a profession, it was only natural that the three of them should know, and befriend, the bouncers that worked in the city. While Helen kept the relationships light and friendly, Peter had ended up sharing a house in one of the northern suburbs with Alan, a muscled, burly man who kept order at one of the most exclusive nightclub venues right in the centre of the city. There was usually no trouble at that club—more rowdy elements stayed away from the higher prices and restrictive dress codes. Maybe that was what convinced Peter that a night covering for his friend, who had food-poisoning, wasn't going to be a problem.

Except it had been.

A group of young men—sons of the rich cattle-farmers that dominated the interior of the state—had come down to Brisbane for a night of fun. Their parents had enough money to ensure thick wallets all around, and they chose the nightclub as the place where they were going to dance and drink away the night. When they got rowdy, the security staff inside the club walked them—quietly but insistently—to the door, and that was where all hell broke loose.

"He was so good," Helen murmured. "The best tae kwon do instructor around." She shook her head.

"It could've happened to anyone, Hel."

She looked up at him then and her eyes blazed. "That's just it though, isn't it, Ryan? Despite his training, it happened to him—just one drunk teenager thinking he was on a rugby field."

The reports afterwards had been chaotic and contradictory, but the police eventually had sorted it all out. After being ejected from the club, the group of young men had started a loud argument with the two bouncers outside. Peter had talked to two of them, trying to get them to calm down, when a third had barrelled into him from the side, knocking him to the kerb. Pete's head had hit the concrete edging next to the road and he'd died instantly.

If Ryan thought she was taking Pete's death hard, he obviously hadn't spoken to Alan recently. Through friends, Helen had learned that Alan was inconsolable over a death he could do nothing to prevent. He'd blamed himself, quit his job and headed back north to his hometown of Townsville. Helen could understand how Alan felt. She was thinking of doing the same kind of thing herself.

"You still thinking of leaving?" It was as if he picked up her thoughts.

She sighed and a sad smile curved her lips. "When I bought my place here, I was so happy. I liked being lulled to sleep by the sound of life and laughter, and didn't even mind being woken up in the morning by the occasional drunk stumbling around outside. It was all part and parcel of living in such a dynamic part of the city. But now, when I hear raised voices or people laughing, it doesn't sound like anyone having fun. It sounds more like how I imagined it must have felt for Pete—just before he got killed. I'm thinking that maybe I've had my fill of Brisbane."

"And where would you go? That place down at Byron?"

Her parents, when they died, had left their holiday home at Byron Bay to Helen and her brother, Nick. Nick, filled with wanderlust as he was, wasn't too interested in maintaining the property. When Helen offered to buy him out of his share, he jumped at the opportunity. He used the money as a launching pad for his travels and now lived happily in northern Italy as a computer programmer. He had come back to visit and spend some time with her once, but admitted that the life of Italian coffee, fresh croissants in the morning, and cobblestoned streets was one that suited him much better than the sea, surf and open spaces of south-east Queensland and northern New South Wales. Maybe, if she could scrape together enough money—and the will to do so—she might pay him a visit.

"Byron Bay has really expanded since my parents bought the property," she countered, knowing Ryan thought of the place as being little more than a hippie commune. "It's a large artist hub, and there are lots of shops, restaurants, and festivals almost year round. I think I could keep myself busy in a place like that."

Ryan snorted. "And what about your business?"

He was referring to Total Defence, the company she started after she left Ryan's academy. Seeing a niche for a mostly female-oriented view of martial arts and self-defence, Helen had started Total Defence as a venture aimed more at companies and groups. In the three years since she'd started, she had already conducted workshops and seminars for a wide range of institutions and women's groups. Occasionally, she also gave private tuition but, although one-on-one sessions were lucrative, they were also physically draining.

"I've spoken to you before about partnering with me," she chided softly. "There's more than enough work. You could take over the Brisbane operation, and I might set up a Byron Bay branch."

"So it's not the work itself that bothers you," he asked, eyeing her intently, "it's just being in Brisbane?"

That wasn't what she'd first told Ryan. In the week following Pete's death, she'd been adamant that she wanted nothing to do with martial arts — after all, if it couldn't save Pete, what good was it? But that was the result of shock and grief. Since then, Helen had taken careful stock of her situation and realised it was the environment itself that caused her the most pain. She loved the work, loved seeing self-confidence blossom in her classes and tracking the progress of her more promising attendees. She also liked the idea of helping men and women protect themselves. Of course, there were always the burly types, who took one look at her slight frame and laughed themselves silly. But those types, she thought with an evil grin, didn't last all that long.

No, teaching people how to protect themselves was in her blood. She could more easily stop breathing than stop her work. Which meant that, despite her love for her hometown, she was going to have to leave it, at least in the short-term.

"Just Brisbane," she agreed. "I'm not saying I won't consider coming back. It's just that I think I need some distance right now."

"And how are your finances?"

Helen frowned as she gazed at him. Her coffee, untouched since that initial sip, was growing cold. It was unlike Ryan to discuss the topic of her moving away with such calm. He hated the idea of her leaving. She had been one of his best students, one of his most personable instructors, and he didn't begrudge her success — in fact, he often drummed up business on her behalf. But if there was one thing he usually point-blank refused to discuss rationally with her, it was her relocating interstate. Whenever the topic came up, he was abrupt, restless and irritable in his remarks and responses. Yet, here he was now, an open expression on his face, asking her on his own initiative about how her plans were going.

"I had to mortgage the apartment to the hilt to get enough money together to buy out Nick's share of the Byron house," she said slowly. "Business is going well but is just paying the expenses at the moment. And I know it's a rising property market, but it would be nice to have a bit of a nest egg to take with me when I move." She narrowed her eyes. "Why are you so interested in my finances all of a sudden?"

He sat back and looked at her smugly. "Because I think I have a way out of your problems."

Chapter Two

Now it was Helen's turn to settle in her chair. She eyed Ryan suspiciously. "What do you mean?"

"I had a funny email request that came through yesterday afternoon."

"Funny, ha-ha. Or funny?" She wriggled her fingers and decided this was exactly the moment to gulp down some lukewarm, milky coffee. For some unknown reason, the hairs on the back of her neck prickled.

He ignored her attempt at humour. "From France," he continued. "Seems some big-shot over there wants to come to Brisbane to do some business."

"To Brisbane?" Helen's voice was incredulous. She loved Brisbane, its relaxed and cosmopolitan air, its varied attractions, but it still didn't hold a candle to the banking powerhouse of Melbourne or the glamour of Sydney. Why would a European businessman choose their little corner of the world?

Ryan shrugged. "That's what he says. His name is," he dug around in his front shirt pocket, pulling out a white, folded piece of paper and opening it up, "er, Guy Aubrac."

"Aubrac," Helen mused out loud. "Can't say I've heard of him."

"Well, from what he wrote, he's looking for," Ryan referred to the slip of paper again, "someone capable, discreet, and socially versatile, who can blend into a variety of social and business environments and still offer top-flight physical protection in case anything goes wrong."

"Like what?"

"I don't know. He doesn't say. Just capable, discreet, and versatile." Ryan refolded the paper and put it back in his pocket. "It's not even a twenty-four by seven job. Just on demand."

She frowned at him. "Does that mean what I think it means?"

Ryan shrugged. "It's the perfect introduction to a solo assignment. They'll probably call you to accompany them to meetings and social events and the rest of the time will be yours. What's there not to like?"

"Will he be expecting a woman?" Helen asked. She didn't kid herself that gender wasn't an important part of security work. People who took orders from a six-foot hunk of muscle sometimes had problems taking the same orders from a five-eight woman.

"He wants someone good, he'll get someone good," the older man dismissed airily. "Who cares if it's a man or woman?"

It looked like her old chief instructor had already made up his mind that she was the right person—the only person—for the task.

"Did they say how long the job was for?"

"Two weeks initially, with the option of extending the assignment at his discretion."

Of course, it was never at the worker's discretion, always the client. Well, considering they were the ones paying the bill, that seemed fair enough.

"And how much money are they offering?"

Ryan looked at her carefully and named a sum that had her sagging in her chair, her mind in a whirl.

"And that's for the two weeks?" she asked faintly.

He nodded.

"Are you sure you got that number right?" she asked. Her voice was a bit breathless from disbelief. "You didn't accidentally add an extra zero to it, did you?"

Ryan looked annoyed, as if he could even be accused of making such a mistake. "I asked for confirmation, and they sent back the same number. It's probably a more reasonable rate in euros, but it adds up to a pretty little sum in Aussie dollars."

The figure Ryan mentioned was more than pretty, it was dazzling. Why, with that kind of money, Helen could take a very comfortable sum with her to Byron—certainly enough to lease or buy her own small building and restart her business there. She wouldn't even have to depend on selling her Fortitude Valley apartment first. The proceeds from this one job were enough to guarantee her independence for at least a year. And all for just two weeks' work.

"It sounds too good to be true," she remarked, trying to find a catch in what she'd been told.

"I asked for a fifty percent deposit," Ryan added. "It hit my account late this morning." He drew out another, slimmer piece of paper and slid it across the table. "This is for you."

With suddenly chilled fingers, Helen reached for the cheque and unfolded it, drawing in a quick breath as she saw her name and the written amount. There were so many zeroes in it! Then her mind kicked in to the implications behind his words.

"You've already set up this whole deal," she accused.

Ryan was unrepentant. "After the first query, we swapped a few more, in between me catching some American football on late-night television. He got on the phone to me around midnight." He paused. "He wanted an answer right away, Hel. What was I supposed to do? Put him on hold while I spent the next hour trying to talk you around?"

She tried to work up some righteous anger, but Ryan's generosity short-circuited all attempts at indignation.

"I took out ten percent," he said, as if wanting to remind her that he really wasn't as soft-hearted as circumstances indicated.

"Yes, I noticed that."

"I thought that was a fair enough commission," he added gruffly.

She nodded. "I'll expect you'll take your commission out of the final payment as well."

"That's right. Business is business."

The side of her mouth curled upwards in a barely repressed smile. Ryan Greenwood hated it if anyone thought there was a heart beating inside that solid chest of his. She was tempted to get up and give him a hug, just to embarrass him.

"So when's my new employer arriving?"

"Tomorrow, he says. He'll be coming with his assistant. They're staying at Heritage House."

Helen's smoke-coloured eyebrows shot upwards. The Heritage House wasn't so much a hotel as a fully-catered two-storey, historical residence on the curving banks of the Brisbane River, just on the edge of the busy city centre. Nestled next to the greenery of one of the city's botanical gardens, it was opulent and discreet, with a private garden that overlooked the river and the cliffs and private multi-level houses of Kangaroo Point on the opposite shore. Helen had gone abseiling on those cliffs several times, and always took time out to gaze at the renovated residence, its severe lines softened by wide verandahs, tropical climbers and hedges of immaculately maintained rose bushes. She wondered which of the four available suites Guy Aubrac was renting.

Ryan correctly interpreted Helen's look of astonishment. "Yeah, the guy must have money coming out of his ears. He wants to meet you tomorrow at eleven."

"In the morning? Won't he be jet-lagged?"

Her ex-instructor shrugged. "I doubt his type get jet-lagged."

Or else he didn't fully realise the kind of distances involved in travelling to Australia. Just flying from one side of the island continent to the other was a trip of more than five hours in a passenger jet. It always confused tourists from smaller countries, who fully expected to drive from, say, Brisbane to Sydney for dinner and then drive back to their hotel again that night!

But it looks so close on the map, they'd wail, and Helen would patiently explain the scale of things in the country, by which stage they'd be wide-eyed and impressed. Perhaps this Guy Aubrac was like that, a savvy businessman in Europe, but ignorant of how large Australia really was.

"All right," she conceded. "Eleven o'clock tomorrow morning at Heritage House. What suite will he be in?"

"Just knock on the door and ask for him. It seems he took the whole house."

For the second time in as many minutes, Helen was stunned. The entire house? That certainly put the amount on her cheque in perspective. Was there anything this man couldn't afford?

"I wonder why he didn't bring his own security with him," she mused. "It looks like he's got enough money to do it."

"I'm not one to look a gift horse in the mouth," Ryan countered. "He wants someone, the job doesn't sound too complicated, and I've nominated you. All you have to do now is stun him with your brilliance, and you're in. And Hel," he added as an afterthought, "you will remember to dress nice, won't you?"

Helen couldn't help herself. She stuck her tongue out at him.

* * * *

Dress nice.

Ryan's words echoed through her head for the rest of the day and the entirety of a sleepless night, but at least it had the advantage of taking her mind off Pete's senseless death for the first time in weeks. She spent the morning sifting through her wardrobe several times, choosing then discarding outfit after outfit. She wanted to appear capable but not too masculine. Discreet, efficient but not aloof.

Screaming her frustration to the ceiling, Helen went through her choices, one more time, and finally decided on an outfit that looked like something an upmarket waiter would wear. Her black pants were slim-fitting but elastic, so they didn't hamper her movements, and she wore medium-heeled patent leather pumps on her feet. Underneath a lightweight, forest green jacket, she didn't wear a blouse, because that was too hot for the climate, but a high-buttoned sleeveless vest with a mandarin collar, made from the same material as her jacket, but in a lighter shade.

She felt—nervous and a bit sick, although why that should be she didn't know. This wasn't the first time she'd met new clients. In fact, she often spoke to a panel of representatives when approaching companies and interest groups. But, for some reason, there was something about this particular assignment—the speed with which it had been organised, the unknown quantity that the client represented, and the ridiculous amount of money involved—that gave her a sense of foreboding.

She caught a taxi to the house and, after paying, walked carefully up the footpath, checking her watch for the twentieth time. Five minutes to eleven. She ran a quick hand down the creaseless jacket and pants. Wriggled her toes in her shoes. Took a breath. And pressed the vintage-styled call button next to the heavy front door of Heritage House.

She didn't hear the bell, but it must have gone off somewhere because barely ten seconds elapsed before she heard the sound of footsteps on the other side of the door and it swung open. A slim, dark-haired woman, obviously one of the staff, smiled at her.

"May I help you?"

"Er, I'm Helen Collier. I have an appointment with Monsieur Guy Aubrac." She let her voice tilt upwards at the end, turning the statement into a bit of a question, but the staff member ushered her in with a slightly puzzled smile.

"I was expecting a Collier, but—" She shook her head. "It doesn't matter. I imagine there's been a bit of a mix-up. Please make your way upstairs, Ms. Collier, and turn left. The meeting room is the first door on your right."

Helen wanted to call her back.

Mix-up? What mix-up? I thought Ryan Greenwood had arranged everything.

But the woman, obviously interrupted by the doorbell, bustled off, leaving Helen alone in the foyer. Black polished granite with white streaks glinted under her feet, and her heels clacked noisily as she walked to the stairs. Thankfully, they were carpeted, the long navy runner held in place by brass stair rods. The pile was thick and Helen's feet sank into it as she ascended.

Turn left and first door on the right, she repeated to herself. The steps at the top ended along a corridor that ran the length of the building, with rooms opening on either side. In front of her, a void opened to the foyer below, and an expanse of windows looked out over the river and the garden below.

This must be where they divided the house, she thought, noticing sets of discreet metal runners inset into the polished timber flooring, one before each wing of rooms began, presumably put there to screen one half of the floor from the other half. There were no partitions in evidence at all, and Helen remembered Ryan telling her that Guy Aubrac had leased the entire building for his own personal use. That was serious money talking.

Helen walked along the suspended corridor and knocked at the first door on her right.

"Entrez," a voice answered. That was French, all right.

She twisted the brass knob and walked in.

There were two men in the room, one sitting in an armchair next to the far wall, overlooking the vista outside, and the other standing just next to the door. The man sitting should, by rights, be the businessman — he looked relaxed and slightly aloof, with dark brown hair and hazel eyes. He regarded her frankly and with a little surprise. But it was the other man who caught and held her attention. This man was tall and well-built, with black hair, olive skin and a piercing pair of icy blue eyes. He hooded them as he watched her, lowering the most sinfully long eyelashes she had ever seen on a man. He must be the assistant, but something told Helen that the one standing was infinitely more dangerous than the man seated on the other side of the room.

"Monsieur Guy Aubrac?" she enquired, looking from one to the other. She hoped they wouldn't ask her any questions in French, because she had just exhausted almost her entire foreign vocabulary with that one word!

"I am Guy Aubrac," the man in the armchair replied. "But who are you, mademoiselle?"

Helen frowned. "I'm Helen Collier. I'm to be your security escort for the next two weeks."

The man who stood to her right shifted impatiently. "There must be some mistake," he said, and his voice was low with a hint of huskiness.

A bedroom voice, Helen thought before she ruthlessly strangled that thought.

"We were expecting a professional, not a little girl! Are you his daughter perhaps?"

Helen stiffened. Although life had become easier for her over the past few years, she still had to battle the inevitable sexism when men thought of ability and martial arts. It looked like she wasn't going to give up the fight any time soon.

She deliberately turned her face away from the tall and disturbing stranger near her and directed all her attention to the man in the armchair.

"I believe you spoke to a colleague of mine?" she asked. "Ryan Greenwood?"

"Oui, this is correct," Guy Aubrac agreed, shrugging. "We sent each other some emails and had a telephone conversation. I informed him of my needs, and he said he had someone eminently suitable."

Helen took a deep breath. "That's me."

"But how can this be?" the taller man interrupted. "We asked for a bodyguard. Not a..." he swept a hand up and down her figure, as if lost for words.

"I must agree with my, er, assistant, Mademoiselle Collier," Aubrac added. "Monsieur Greenwood told me a Monsieur 'Hell' Collier would be meeting with us this morning. At the time, I admit I was a bit concerned by such an evocative nickname, but the Greenwood name is highly respected."

Helen wasn't surprised. The number of people worldwide connected with martial arts that Ryan didn't know could be counted on the fingers of one hand. He'd be happy to have that snippet of news passed onto him. But that still didn't get her out of her current predicament. She wondered darkly if Ryan had deliberately misled the two Frenchmen, or if it was due to a genuine miscommunication.

"My name is Helen Collier," she told them. "Hel, with one 'l', for short."

"And what of your father?" The tall, disturbing one asked.

"Dead," she answered succinctly, looking him full in the face, daring him to contradict her.

The corner of that sensuous mouth twitched at her tone. "And do you have any brothers?"

"One. Overseas."

"Uncles?" he asked with a lift of an eyebrow.

"My father was an only child."

"So no nephews?"

"None." She enunciated the word as clearly as she could.

They stared at each other for several long moments. Helen couldn't tell exactly, but there was something about the man that irritated her intensely. Irritated her and tempted her to rip off his clothes, right there and then, and run her tongue down the taut flesh of the muscled body she knew lay under the long-sleeved business shirt. What would he look like in the throes of passion, with that superior smirk wiped from his face? She was dying to know.

Someone cleared their throat, and Helen was brought back to reality with a thump. She flushed and turned to face her prospective employer, hoping that she hadn't just irretrievably wrecked her chances at the assignment. Think of the money Hel, she told herself, and keep your mouth shut.

"This is a very large misunderstanding, Maidemoiselle Collier."

Aubrac shook his head from side to side, and Helen's heart dropped to the floor. She had really done it this time—turned a sweet gig into a disaster. Ryan was going to have a field day with what she had just managed to do. Her dreams of moving to Byron Bay sometime within the next decade died a swift death.

"I'm afraid I have," Aubrac flicked a glance at his assistant then suddenly spluttered into a coughing fit. He thumped his chest a couple of times before continuing. "I mean, I, er, was wondering if there is a way that, er, you could illustrate your competence."

"An exhibition of my skills, you mean?"

"Oui. Yes. An exhibition."

This was better. Helen was on more familiar ground with a request like that. People never liked to think that a slim, young woman could pound someone bigger and heavier into the ground, and she often had to prove herself to win contracts. She could win this one, she thought with sudden determination. She always did.

"On who?" she asked. "You?"

"How about me?" that low, molten voice interrupted.

A smile slowly formed on Helen's face.

* * * *

For the first time in his adult life, Yves didn't know what to think. He had worked out a small ploy—it wasn't anything that would deter anybody who knew either of them well, but would serve to grant them a little extra peace. For the moment—and only for the moment—he and Guy would trade places. He would be the assistant, and Guy would be the high-profile, super-rich businessman in need of some discreet security.

But when that girl—non! That woman—had walked through the door, Yves had felt something catch in his throat, making it difficult to breathe. He had met confident women before, but this slim scrap exuded a self-assurance that he had only seen in men decades older. Her black trousers clung to her legs and thighs, and what Yves saw, as his gaze raced up her figure, was slender and enticing, until the rest was hidden by the hem of an embroidered green jacket. He knew it wasn't an haute couture piece, but the needlework indicated this was still a valuable, one-off item of clothing, probably sewn by a local designer. It was a perfect fit on Helen Collier's body, tucking in to emphasise a trim waist before flaring over a pair of most feminine hips.

Helen Collier, not Hell Collier.

Yves wasn't sure whether the mistake was made by Ryan Greenwood, a highly-recommended and discreet personal security expert, who had served several of his close friends, or by Guy himself. Whatever the case, he had arrived in Brisbane, expecting a grizzled and experienced man — much like Ryan Greenwood himself — and, instead, was confronted by one of the most perplexingly attractive women he'd ever met.

His gaze wandered over her face, taking the opportunity to look at her more closely while she traded words with Guy. Her hair was severely scraped back from her forehead and held in place by a pair of long clips, but he knew she found it an ongoing struggle to control those sun-kissed, curly blonde locks. Even as he looked, an errant tendril snapped free of its restraint and fell, caressing her cheek. Her skin was smooth and glowing, dotted with pale freckles, and her eyes were large and candid, accentuated by the darker, delicate eyebrows winging above each of them. Only her mouth — a sweetly pink cupid's bow when at rest, but tightened with determination at the moment — commanded more attention, begging to be kissed and sucked until it moaned in pleasure.

He tuned into the conversation in time to suggest himself as a potential guinea pig, and was amused and gratified by the brief frisson of alarm that danced across her features. That was good. It showed she wasn't unaware of him and of the sneaking attraction that wound its way around them both.

Pinning a small smile on his face, he stood there, watching as she skimmed his figure from head to toe. Why, even in those shiny black shoes of hers, she must only reach to his shoulders. But then he saw the look in her eyes and felt a stab of unease. The young woman looked at him as if…as if he was nothing more than a slab of meat! A filet de boeuf on display at a butcher's counter, to be analysed and prodded before being either chosen or discarded, her gaze cool and assessing. It was as though she was weighing him for some purpose, and Yves was uncomfortably struck by the thought that he probably had a similar expression on his face when gazing at beautiful women.

Mon dieu, was that true? He thought he treated each of his bed partners with cordiality and respect, but this detached appraisal brought home the other side of the coin — of women he had eyed in the casinos and on the racing circuits and polo fields of Europe — and a shiver of unease crawled up Yves' spine, making him shrug his shoulders in order to relax his muscles again.

Who was this petite femme who dared look at him in such a manner, he wondered with growing irritation. He would send her packing and have stern words with Ryan Greenwood after this. The Australian would be lucky to get another international client again. Yves flexed his shoulders again, this time more casually. He might be a businessman, but he had been an athletic young man, even trying out for the French soccer team while he was still studying at university. His ongoing fitness was something he took very seriously. He jerked his head up. So let's see how many seconds it would take before this young scrap found herself on the floor and out of a very lucrative contract.

"Would you like me to keep the jacket on or off?" she asked, lightly.

"Off," he said shortly, then realised that both people were staring at his quick and abrupt response. He smiled, softening the words. "This part of the world is quite warm. I doubt you'll need to wear many warm clothes. Let us dress for the weather in this demonstration."

She nodded and unbuttoned the jacket. It was a simple and casual series of gestures, but watching her nimble fingers as she snapped each button free was one of the most erotic things Yves had seen in his life. She shrugged off the garment and walked to the empty chair next to Guy, laying it carefully over the chair's back, while he rolled up the sleeves of his shirt. The top that looked so demure while under the jacket revealed itself to be a smooth, short sheath of glistening sensuality. The vest hugged Helen Collier's curves even more lovingly than the jacket did, and Yves slowly let out a silent breath. Even Guy watched her with obvious male appreciation. Then she turned back to him, and he concentrated once more on the lesson at hand.

"What would you like me to show you?" she asked of Guy.

He waved in his assistant's direction. "Um, Monsieur Nerin will let you know."

If the young woman thought it strange that a rich man referred to his assistant in the formal manner, she made no comment.

She looked at him enquiringly but he shrugged, his mind completely — and uncharacteristically — empty.

"Okay, why not pretend you have a knife?" she suggested. "Take a stab at me."

He didn't believe she was ready. She couldn't be ready, not when she had not adopted any traditional stance that he knew. Her feet were a little apart, but she had not even raised her hands. Maybe this femme didn't know anything, and this whole episode was some kind of sick dare aimed at an unsuspecting foreign dupe. Well, she would soon find out what it meant to waste the time of Yves de Saint Nerin!

Despite his irritation, Yves didn't want to hurt her so, imaginary knife in hand, he made a relatively slow overhand lunge at her with his right hand. He didn't know what happened next, although Guy told him later that she moved the instant he started his downward arm movement. There was a stinging pain in his arm, then across his chest, then he felt a hard wall slam into his back. The breath whooshed out of him.

Helen Collier stepped up and glared at him. "Only villains in television dramas try to knife someone in an overhand attack," she told him. "How about attempting something a bit sneakier?"

Yves grimaced and tried hard not to look too flustered. He stepped forward, away from the wall, and she stepped back to give him more room. He glanced over at Guy, who looked like he was trying to hold back spasms of laughter.

He was distracted, that was all. Distracted by that revealing figure-hugging vest item she was wearing, and a fragrance that reminded him of a summer's breeze blowing across French fields. He would not make that same mistake again.

He frowned at Guy, to show that he was not happy to be the butt of someone's joke, and asked for the pen that lay on a table next to his assistant. Guy threw it to him, and he caught it with one hand. That felt better. Now he could better visualise what it would be like to be holding a weapon, instead of just pretending to. That was another thing that probably threw him off, simulating a knife attack without a knife. Feeling more confident, Yves widened his stance and opened his arms, beckoning her to fall into his embrace. This was certainly something different for him, enfolding a woman in a way that was not at all affectionate.

Helen didn't move. She just stood there, waiting, looking at him with those huge, stormy eyes until he eventually took a step forward, determined to try for a slash across her body this time. Again, she moved faster than he could track. He felt something hard contact his hand, sending the pen spinning across the room, then a sharp elbow in his gut, driving the air from his body. This time, he felt himself stagger back, hitting the wall once again. Dimly, he heard Guy spluttering in the distance, but he shook his head. In front of him, Helen Collier stood, as cool and unruffled as before.

Bien, so the chit knew something after all. But Yves was still not willing to put his safety in her delicate looking hands.

"That was an impressive demonstration, Madame Collier," Guy said, obviously thinking that Yves had had enough of being slammed into a wall. "I think perhaps we have seen–"

"Non," Yves interrupted loudly. "Let's clear some space and try one more time. And not with a pretend, or otherwise, knife this time."

Something flickered across her face—it couldn't possibly be amusement—and then she was helping Guy move the furniture to the other side of the room. The conference table was rather large, but they turned it sideways and shoved it against the wall, leaving a large open space near the door for Yves' last experiment. Despite himself, he liked that about her. There was no hesitation in helping Guy, even when it involved moving heavy objects around the room. The usual women of his acquaintance would have shrieked horribly lest they chip one of their perfectly manicured fingernails but, after slanting that one sly look at him, she had pitched in without complaint. It was—disconcertingly attractive.

But he was not here to run an admiring glance over his supposed bodyguard. He was here to prove that she simply didn't have what it took to take care of him. There was nothing personal in the thought. He didn't mind women around, of course, but in their proper places—and with one so attractive, on a hair-trigger as she walked by his side, there was no such place. But maybe, after he convinced her that they could not deal together, she might still be open for dinner as a consolation prize. While he was determined to remain in Australia till the police had time to thoroughly investigate Leonid Alexandrov, nobody said the time he spent here had to be celibate.

He smiled disarmingly as he faced her, but nothing so much as flickered behind those cool, assessing eyes. D'accord!

He moved with a panther's grace, feinting in one direction then stepping in another, and had the satisfaction of seeing sudden surprise on her face

47

before it was quickly masked. He didn't have time to wonder why such a thought gratified him before he lunged at her again, this time catching her wrist in a vice-like grip. He expected her to scream, to say something, to stop, but she kept moving as if it didn't matter that he held onto her in the kind of hold, he was sure, she could not break.

To his own surprise, she angled around to his back and he felt a stab of pain in his kidneys. He had no choice, he had to let go of her hand — the strike to his back both stunned and hurt him — and he felt a quick kick to the back of his knees.

He was still surprised as he felt himself falling, her hand on him — touching him, moving with him like a lover — as he fell through the air and hit the carpet. When he opened his eyes, she was crouched above him. Her hand tightened against his throat, fingers like steel cables against his neck, and one of her feet pinned down his right arm. He knew he could play the macho man now, and sweep her aside just as she'd managed to demonstrate her skills without hurting him too much, turning the tables on her and sneering in her face. Something in her face told him she half-expected him to do exactly that, and he was ashamed that she thought so little of his gender.

He relaxed his body, ceding defeat, and tried smiling up at her. This was no mean feat, considering she was still pressing her fingers against his windpipe, but it was enough, and she relaxed her hold and swiftly moved away from him, rising to her feet.

"Would that be enough of a demonstration, Monsieur Nerin?" she asked, unable to keep the silkiness out of her voice.

"Oui," he replied, although he had the urge to cough. "You're hired."

Chapter Three

Oh, he felt good. Helen half-curled her fingers into her palms as she stepped away from Mr. Nerin. Maybe she had hit him a little harder than she should have—that mocking look on his face had goaded her into proving herself once and for all—but he was as hard and delicious to the touch as she'd known he would be. It was difficult laying a hand on him to move him when all she wanted to do was grab him and pull him closer, and press those cynical lips of his against hers. In a way, the demonstration made it more difficult, because she now had the memory of his body imprinted on her fingertips, and his dark and spicy masculine aroma seared into her brain.

With a tight smile at both men, she walked to the vacant armchair and shrugged into her jacket, buttoning it up. She usually didn't care about such things—she had a job to do and that was the most important thing—but there was a driving need to hide herself from the tall man who now watched her with a glint of speculation in his eye. She felt vulnerable in front of him, as if he could somehow see straight into her soul, and she didn't like it.

And that wasn't the only thing bothering her. The relationship between the two men was somehow out of balance. Mr. Nerin seemed to hold the upper hand, even though he was supposedly Guy Aubrac's assistant. It wasn't just his height, but his personality that commanded automatic respect. She stood relaxed and looked at the businessman. He'd think it was because she expected a final answer from him — after all, he was the one paying her — but she was actually using those seconds to weigh up his character. Maybe he was one of those men who inherited his money from a line of wealthy ancestors. And, rather than admit that he had little business acumen himself, had set about hiring the most astute assistant he could find. Helen didn't know how such things played out in Europe, but it sounded possible to her. What a stroke of luck then that he had managed to find Mr. Nerin. The man didn't even have to speak to have everyone scurrying about, doing his nonverbal bidding. One flick from his eyebrow, or a glare from those deep, mysterious, blue eyes of his, and lesser mortals would instantly divine what was wrong and rush to rectify whatever had displeased him.

The explanation seemed plausible to Helen, except for the fact that no-first-name gorgeous hunk didn't look the type to bend his will to any other person. Even when she had him on the floor, pinned with one foot and ready to do some serious damage to his throat with the other, he was the one who told her she was hired, while his employer sat across the room, frozen into inaction, unwilling to cut the demonstration short. Could Guy Aubrac see the unstoppable ambition in his assistant? Helen hoped so, because Mr. Nerin was, quite simply, lethal, and Guy seemed too nice a person to be drowned by the tsunami of his assistant's obvious zeal.

"That was, er, a very formidable demonstration, Madame. I think," he glanced over at the other man who was—Helen was amused to hear—coughing discreetly behind her, "we can safely say you are hired for this position."

"I have something to say to Monsieur Aubrac," Nerin added, his voice still a bit raspy from her hold on his throat. "If you could just step out of the room for a moment?"

It wasn't a request even though it sounded like one. Helen nodded her head and left the room, closing the door behind her with a soft click.

What in the world was wrong now? Had she somehow dented Nerin's pride, and he was now after revenge? Was he going to suggest that they reverse the decision to hire her? But he seemed to concede the situation earlier. Helen's hands became suddenly clammy, and she paced back and forth, in front of the door with short, quick steps. She hated having her future determined by someone else, and she hated the fact that she was desperate for the money that was on offer. It would solve so many of her more immediate problems. But all of her plans would remain fantasy if she couldn't somehow convince the two men in the room that she could be trusted with their personal security.

The door swung open noiselessly, and she looked up into a pair of blue eyes. Whatever Helen had done to him, he looked completely recovered. A polite, but impervious, expression was on his face, and she met a wall when she tried to dig deeper, to find out what he was thinking behind such a blankly civil gaze. She couldn't tell whether she was going to get the job, or be thrown out on her ear. And she couldn't tell if he was as disturbed by their intimate encounter as she still was.

"Please come in."

Helen entered the room, hoping her anxiety wasn't too obvious. Mr. Nerin moved past her—she got another whiff of his delectable fragrance—to the other armchair and seated himself. Both men looked at her.

Aubrac cleared his throat. "May I ask where you live, Madame?"

It was strange how uncomfortable he looked as he asked that question, as if it had been reluctantly pulled from him.

"Fortitude Valley," she replied, then realised that the two foreigners might not know where that was. "It's north of the city but quite close to here. It's no trouble getting here each day, if that's what you're asking."

The slight pink on Guy Aubrac's face deepened, puzzling her. "We would, ah, prefer it if you stayed here. At our expense, of course," he added quickly.

She looked around. "At Heritage House?"

The thought was tempting. Actually, it was more than tempting. The opportunity to live in the lap of luxury in an historic and impeccably renovated house with a million-dollar view—the object of her abseiling fantasies—was almost irresistible. Almost.

"But why?" she continued, quashing down her errant thought. "I live only a handful of minutes

53

away." She thought back to the coffee she'd shared with Ryan yesterday, and his assurance that she wouldn't be needed around the clock.

"If you're going anywhere, I can be here—dressed appropriately—in less than twenty minutes," she persisted.

"But what if m-Monsieur Aubrac's schedule is more spontaneous?" Nerin asked smoothly.

"I still don't see the problem," she countered. "Is a wait of ten or twenty minutes really going to make much of a difference?"

Nerin glared at her, obviously bothered by her stubbornness.

Why was she making such a big issue out of this, Helen wondered to herself. Most people would jump at the chance to stay at the historic home, especially if it didn't cost them a cent. But the truth was, she didn't really want to be any closer to the disturbing Mr. Nerin than she absolutely had to be. There was something about the man that constantly unsettled her, from his frankly assessing gaze to the leashed power of his body. Not to mention the feel of his hot, taut muscles under her fingers, a disloyal part of her added.

"It may do," the object of her musings replied in clipped tones. "And what if I, or Monsieur Aubrac, are attacked? Do we say to them, could you please wait until our bodyguard arrives?"

His voice was mocking and Helen flushed at the taunt.

"I would have thought, Madame Collier that, considering what we are prepared to pay you, a bit of loyalty to your employer is not out of the question."

Damn him, but the man was right. Under any other circumstances, Helen wouldn't have hesitated. It was quite natural for a client to want his security escort close by, and staying at Heritage House was no hardship. And, besides... She. Needed. That. Money.

"You are correct, Monsieur Nerin," she finally conceded stiffly. "I will make arrangements to move into Heritage House tomorrow."

"Today," he said firmly.

Even her ostensible employer, Guy Aubrac, looked surprised at that.

"Today?" she repeated.

"We have paid for two weeks of your time, have we not?"

"Y-e-s.".

He nodded, as if the discussion was already closed. "And today is part of that two weeks. Therefore, you will move in today."

There was nothing she could say to that, except stare at him blankly.

"Tell me where you live, and I shall help you move."

Let this man into her private apartment? Her private life? Only if she had a death wish! The one thing she was absolutely sure of, was the fact that Monsieur Nerin was unforgettable. As things stood, she knew she would never scale the rocky wall at Kangaroo Point again without remembering her meeting here today. She would never be able to enter Heritage House, or look at pictures of it, without being reminded of his intense, blue eyes or the feel of his body against hers.

"I, I don't think that's necessary," she stammered.

"You are on m—our time, Madame. I want to make sure we get our money's worth from this engagement."

"It's not as though I live across the ocean, Monsieur," she shot back, stressing the title slightly. "If I forget something, I can go back and get it quite easily."

"I expect you to be here twenty-four hours by seven days. That is the condition of our agreement."

"And I only live ten minutes away!"

They stood, glaring at each other. Finally, he dropped his gaze, flicking a glance at his watch. "It is now ten-thirty. We will have a briefing at eleven-thirty to explain my—and Monsieur Aubrac's—requirements. Will that give you enough time to move your things?"

He made it sound as though whatever she did was of no consequence, and Helen gritted her teeth. If only she didn't need this job so badly. And only an hour to get home, pack, come back, and then attend a meeting? If it was anybody else, she would have asked for extra time—even an additional thirty minutes would do—but she was not going to request any favours from this arrogant foreigner. Not when he had made it abundantly clear that he and his employer had essentially bought her, round the clock, for two weeks.

"More than enough," she replied. "In which case, I should be on my way now." She lifted an eyebrow in as haughty a manner as she could manage, but he didn't seem to notice.

"Bien. We'll see you in one hour."

* * * *

"Of all the arrogant," Helen threw a pair of trousers into the smallest suitcase she could find, "inconsiderate," two blouses, "arrogant," she repeated, her hand bunching the material of a dress she held. She looked at it, took a deep breath, and turned the suitcase upside down, dumping the contents back on her bed. This was not, she admitted ruefully, a mature way to deal with the situation.

Smoothing the dress, she started again, quickly folding it into one neat flat bundle and placing it at the bottom of her case. Her hands worked methodically, folding and placing, while her mind raced.

Maybe Ryan should be the one she slow-roasted over an open fire. After all, he was the one who got her into this mess in the first place. But she had dived in willingly, seduced by the thought of so much money for only a few days' work. She picked a sun-dress from her closet, looked at it critically, then folded it and added it to the growing pile in the bag. She had better stop before she overstuffed it. All that was left was to pack some lingerie, and that was it, and all—she glanced quickly at the wall clock—just before eleven o'clock, too. She should make it back to the meeting in plenty of time.

But when Helen got to the drawer of her dresser, and pulled it open, she paused, looking at its contents in dismay. There was nothing frivolous or frilly in anything she owned—the underwear was comfortable and cotton, in a variety of dusky tones, none of which screamed sexy to anyone, and her bras were serviceable and staid, bought to look unobtrusive under a variety of clothes.

She slowly sank onto the corner of her bed. Not a fire-engine red teddy, thong, or low-cut lacy bra in sight. Just a crush of sensible items, pushed chaotically into a drawer. Nothing to draw and seduce a member of the opposite sex. Not that she disliked sex. As a matter of fact, she enjoyed it very much. It was just that the men she had dated so far seemed more interested in dominating her completely in bed, as if that somehow balanced the relationship between them. She thought she would have liked to fall in love with a romantic — a man with steady eyes and a calm and gentle manner — but, in truth, such men were the first to run away from her, misreading her self-confidence as arrogance. The only men who weren't afraid to approach her were overbearing and over-confident, two traits that definitely turned her off.

So, why then, when the irritating Mr. Nerin seemed to fit into that category so well, was she disappointed that she had nothing vampish to take with her to Heritage House? It couldn't be that she actually wanted him to run his lean fingers over her body, could it? She shook her head in dismay. What would Ryan say if he knew what she was thinking? He had set her up for the assignment of a lifetime, and all she could think of was jumping into bed with her employer's assistant! This was not the way a professional behaved.

Helen blindly scooped up an armful of items from the drawer and dumped it on top of the case, zipping it shut. She was not going to indulge in fantasies of doing the wild thing with assistant Nerin while she was staying at Heritage House, she told herself as she checked that the windows were securely closed and took the large, creaky elevator to the ground floor. She found a taxi at the nearby rank and settled back in the seat as it sped its way to the centre of the city. She was not going to let him get under her skin so easily. She was going to behave like the consummate professional she knew herself to be. She was going to get through the two weeks, skip away with a fat cheque in her hands and move to Byron Bay with a light heart and a clear head.

The trip took less time than she wanted but longer than she needed, and time was ticking as she was shown to one of the downstairs suites. She didn't even have time to take a proper look around. She dropped her case on the carpeted floor and ran up the stairs, knocking on that dreaded meeting room door with a little less than five minutes to spare. There was a moment's pause, which gave her time to catch her breath, before she was asked to enter.

The furniture had been moved to the room's original configuration, and the large rectangular table was back to its dominating position in the middle of the room. At one end, Guy sat, with Mr. Nerin at his side. Did they mean for her to walk the length of the table and sit close to them? Helen was afraid she'd be much too close to Guy Aubrac's assistant if she did that so, with an inclination of her head, she took the chair at the opposite end. A gleam of amusement glinted in Nerin's eye before disappearing quickly.

"We should get the protocols sorted out first," he began, with not even an acknowledgement that she had arrived on time. Damn the man, but she should start remembering that he was going to be a huge disappointment if she expected anything from him that remotely resembled manners.

"During our stay here, we want to fit into the local scenery as much as possible."

Really? Although Guy Aubrac was an attractive man, and would undoubtedly garner some feminine attention wherever he went, Mr. Nerin was another matter completely. He had roughly the same chance of disappearing into the woodwork as a Bird of Paradise in a hen-house.

"So, from now on, we will try to dispense with the French formalities. While you will continue calling, er, your employer 'Mr. Aubrac', you may call me, Yves."

Yves. She rolled it around her head, liking the way he drew the pronunciation of his name out and noting how easily it could be whispered in the heat of passion. The sudden thought made her flush, and it deepened when she noticed a blue gaze locked onto hers. She cleared her throat and shifted in her chair.

"That sounds fine." She tested the two titles out aloud. "Mr. Aubrac. Yves."

"Do you have any questions for us?" Yves asked, a dark eyebrow lifting.

Of course she had questions. As a security escort, she should be full of questions. Up till now, Ryan had handled that side of the business, roping her in when he needed extra hands, or someone to relieve him. She thought furiously of the kinds of questions the head of a security firm might ask.

"What brings you to Brisbane, Mr. Aubrac?" she asked, making her voice sound brisk but friendly. "It's a long way from France."

"We are looking at business interests here," he answered with a smile. "M-my firm is thinking of expanding into this region, and we are due to hold a series of meetings over the next two weeks with a company called Tec-"

"Is knowing the name of a company with which we are thinking of doing business of critical need to you, Ms. Collier?" Yves interrupted.

"Please," she said, "call me Helen."

He nodded but stayed quiet, waiting for an answer.

"I think that's a most relevant detail," she hesitated briefly, "Yves. Ensuring your safety while you are out near Alice Springs, inspecting an installation of some kind, for example, would need a different strategy to, say, buying a bank in the middle of the city."

Yves looked at her while his fingers drummed the top of the table, then his shoulders relaxed. "Very well. We're here to speak with the managers of a company called Tech-88. Have you heard of them?"

She shook her head.

"They are a small but promising software company with several lucrative contracts in this region. We aim to offer them a partnership, capital and exposure to the European market in return for a foothold here in the Asia-Pacific region."

"And they're based here in Brisbane?"

"That's correct."

It all sounded very logical, but Helen hadn't thought of the computer software business as being so cut-throat before. What other reason was there for hiring a bodyguard for what was only supposed to be a series of meetings?

"You must have rivals then?" she suggested, following her train of thought.

"Rivals?" Yves looked affronted, as if nobody dared compete with him. "There may be, but they're irrelevant to the current negotiations."

She frowned. "No competition hoping to," she made an ironing gesture with her hand, "rub you out?"

"Rub—?" His face cleared. "Oh, you mean wishing to injure us? No, I believe we're quite safe from any potential competitors."

"Then why, Mr. Aubrac," she asked deliberately, "are you employing me?"

Both sets of male eyes snapped to her.

"You've just told me that you have no competitors for this deal," she explained. "And I seriously doubt a bunch of manic programmers are about to hunt you down with microchips. So why do you need me for your security work?"

"Because," Guy Aubrac started blinking hard and sent an entreating look to his assistant, "that is–"

"Mr. Aubrac is a very successful businessman," Yves interjected smoothly. "This deal may not pose any personal danger to him, but there could be people from previous negotiations, who wish him harm. Sore losers, I believe you term them."

The man had all the answers, Helen concluded. He was quick and glib, but there was something still not right about the whole situation. Could she imagine a man like Aubrac ruthlessly conducting business deals, so much so that a rival might be tempted to harm him? No, she couldn't. Guy Aubrac was a serious young man, but he was pleasant and even a bit breezy, when he wasn't looking perplexed or

Guarding His Body

confused. If anybody had to fear for his life, it was someone like Yves Nerin, with his clipped, no-nonsense tone and haughty manner. She could very easily imagine the driving urge to get revenge on Yves—without even thinking of business rivals, a whole gaggle of ex-girlfriends probably made it part of their daily affirmation before they put their make-up on.

"So what exactly will my duties entail?" she asked.

"Of course, we will want you to accompany Mr. Aubrac on his meetings with the management of Tech-88."

"Of course," she murmured.

"And, other than that, I shall direct you in whatever tasks are necessary."

"You?" She tried—failed—to keep thick reluctance from her voice. "But aren't I employed by Mr. Aubrac? Shouldn't I be taking orders from him?"

Meanwhile, the object of her objection sat there, silent and mesmerised, watching the match between her and Yves with open fascination.

"You forget, Helen." A shiver danced up her spine as he spoke her name softly. "I am Mr. Aubrac's personal assistant. I am the one who plans his day, down to the last second."

Helen gazed into his eyes and knew when she was defeated. "I understand."

"Were there any other questions?" he asked.

"I'm sure we can discuss further details later on." She got to her feet. "If you gentlemen will excuse me, I'll go unpack my case."

With a sigh of relief, she let herself out of the room and headed for the stairs. But her peace wasn't to last long. A set of quick, muffled steps dogged her, and she groaned inwardly. That could only be one of two people, and she doubted it was the affable Mr. Aubrac. She tried to ignore the male presence behind her as she headed for her ground-floor suite, hoping he was on his way to the kitchen with some special order for lunch or something. His footsteps disappeared in the opposite direction.

That was only a temporary reprieve, she told herself. Remember not to lose your temper. This man obviously has the power to terminate your contract, and that's the last thing you want to happen.

She slid open the door to her suite and walked down the timber-lined corridor. The passage opened into a large living/dining area, decorated with heavy timber furniture that gleamed from the amount of polishing it had obviously undergone. Protecting the top of the solid dining table was a thick piece of glass. The living room furniture consisted of overstuffed sofas. They were designed in the traditional style, but the leather was soft and supple, and they looked cosy and comfortable. Next to the dining area was a small kitchen and, from a brief glance, it looked fully-stocked. Warm-hued tea towels hung from a series of hooks at its entrance, just above the breakfast bar.

Helen looked to her left, out to the garden, river and a cityscape of Brisbane. The view, already lovely, would look breathtaking at night, with the lights from the tall office buildings sparkling like giant columns of fairy lights. The large living area narrowed into another corridor at the far end, and three doors led off it—two bedrooms and a bathroom. Helen hadn't been in the bathroom yet but, if the rest of the suite was any indication, she was sure it would be well-appointed and opulent. She entered the bedroom that overlooked the garden, and sighed as she took in the large French windows and wide verandah. Two squatter's chairs were already positioned outside in welcome, the frames made of solid timber, the upholstery a textured, creamy ivory, and the wooden leg-rests were swung out, waiting for a relaxation-minded guest. Maybe later she would try one out.

But, for now, her case lay discarded on the coverlet of a four-poster king-sized bed, looking tiny and forlorn. She smiled and unzipped the top flap, lifted an armful of the lingerie she had thrown in last, turned to the dresser...and froze in shock.

Watching her—leaning against the door jamb as if he had nothing better to do—was Yves himself. He looked around the room, as if admiring the interior decoration, and gave her a lazy smile. Helen's heart thumped hard in her chest, and she closed her eyes when she realised exactly what she held in her arms. Of course, he would have to be there in time to see the dowdy and sensible underclothes she chose for herself. She knew she should have been indignant—he hadn't even so much as knocked at the entrance to her suite or otherwise indicated he was invading her territory—but, instead, she was sorely embarrassed. She snapped open her eyes. Damn. He was still there.

Turning away, she bent over and jiggled a dresser drawer open with one hand, dumped in her lingerie unceremoniously, and closed the drawer with a thud. If she was trying to send him a message, he blithely ignored it.

"What are you doing here?" she demanded, narrowing her eyes.

"This suite is very nice," he said, making a show of looking around. She took advantage of the fact he turned to scan the living room to slip past him, forcing him to continue the conversation in a less intimate room.

"Was there something I could help you with, er, Yves?" That name sounded too personal, too intimate on her lips.

"I thought I could help carry your case," he said with a careless shrug. "It might have been heavy."

She blinked at him in disbelief. She had hit this man — three times — sent him crashing against the wall and then to the floor. She had put her hand around his throat, partially choking his air supply. She had moved furniture around in the meeting room. And he was here, offering help to lift a small suitcase? She didn't know whether to be insulted or amused.

A reluctant smile tugged at her lips.

"I only brought enough for a week," she replied, feeling a bit more relaxed. "The case wasn't that heavy."

He nodded, but still made no move to leave.

"Was there something else?" she asked.

His mind was lost somewhere else. She knew it, because he took such a long time to answer her — well, long for him, especially when she was already used to his rapid-fire responses. He focused slowly back on her then cleared his throat self-consciously, and that somehow made him seem more human and even slightly endearing.

"I just wanted to tell you that you are free for the rest of the day while G–Mr. Aubrac and I finalise the meeting schedule with Tech-88. A buffet lunch will be served in the garden. What are you doing for dinner?" he asked suddenly.

"Dinner. I hadn't really thought about it." The morning had passed in such a whirlwind that Helen was sure it was a harbinger of the days to come. She wasn't expecting to have much time to herself.

"Then it's agreed. You'll join me for dinner. Shall we say, seven o'clock?"

"Join you?" There he went again. Just when Helen was starting to warm to him, he turned all arrogant European on her and made her want to hit him. Again.

"Mais oui. We will be working together, will we not? Surely it's best for us to get along for the duration of this assignment?"

"What about Mr. Aubrac? Won't he be expecting—"

"Mr. Aubrac usually prefers to dine alone," Yves interjected smoothly.

Helen wasn't convinced. "I don't think—"

He stepped close, and she could smell him again, that intriguing mix of after-shave and Yves. Helen knew she should push him away, avoiding him like she did in the meeting room upstairs, but she was rooted to the spot.

"There are prickles," he said softly, and his voice was like a physical caress. To her intense embarrassment, Helen felt herself get wet just listening to the words. Oh God, how she wanted to throw herself into his arms and feel his hands stroke her the way his words seemed to. This is not the way to behave, she told herself, but her body wasn't listening. His gaze was enough to send her nipples puckering into small, hard nubs.

"But underneath," he continued, "there is passion, I think. Much passion."

She didn't even know that she'd taken a step forward. Once again, her body was acting independently of her cautious mind. It was as though he had cast a spell over her. But if she thought she was the only one affected, a small part of her was relieved to note that he seemed equally caught in the snare of attraction that sizzled between them. He angled his head, his lips met hers, and Helen combusted.

Oh, this is so wrong, she thought in despair, even as she succumbed to his embrace. It was only her first day on assignment, and already she had fallen for her employer's assistant. At least, it wasn't her employer—heaven knew how she would ever justify that to herself—but it was still wrong.

She tried pulling away, but his hands around her were like bands of steel, holding her tight. It appeared that whatever affliction affected her was affecting him as well. Their kiss, partner to the embrace, heated Helen's blood, making her push her body against his hard planes and mould her curves around the shaft of hard flesh she felt against her belly. He groaned deep in his throat, ravishing her mouth, teasing her tongue before reluctantly drawing away. But he didn't have the control he wished. Helen could tell from his ragged breathing and the dilation of his eyes—not to mention the evidence that had pressed against her belly only moments ago—that he was still a hairsbreadth from losing control completely.

"D'accord," he finally murmured, after clearing his throat. "Seven it is. I shall see you then."

And he walked out of the room before she could say a word.

Chapter Four

It shouldn't be this difficult.

Helen frowned as she regarded the small selection of clothes in her new wardrobe. For one, she was angry. After the big rush to get her moved into a suite at Heritage House, suddenly she found she literally had hours on her hands. As promised, a small buffet lunch had been laid out in the garden, but, after grabbing mounded plates of food, both Yves and Mr. Aubrac had disappeared into the house again, leaving Helen to work her way through a solitary meal. Not that she didn't enjoy it. The food was wonderful, the weather was warm and breezy, and the view was superb. But, damn it all, couldn't they have just had that meeting with her straight after the interview, told her about lunch, then let her go back to her apartment to pack in peace?

For two, there was also Yves' unbelievable high-handedness. Helen could have told him that such arrogance did not impress her. She had met many men who somehow thought it was their God-given right to dictate a woman's actions, and the schedule for those actions. But…

But, but, but.

There was something else about Yves Nerin. Something playful amidst the sternness, something charming despite the hauteur. Something — she didn't know how to describe it exactly — that set him apart. She had seen handsome men before, so it wasn't as though only his exotically dark looks turned her head. Maybe it was the way he had come to ask if he could help her with her case, even though she had just nearly wiped the floor with him. Most men of her past acquaintance would have left her to it, with a pithy comment about women's rights. But not Yves. He was charming and courteous with a surprising sense of humour.

And that was even before she considered that kiss. It overshadowed everything else. But what did it mean, especially when he seemed to accord her no more than a casual glance over the lunch table? Had she imagined the unmistakable sign of his arousal? Or maybe he didn't want to show any sign of his desire in front of his employer. That made sense. Although Yves Nerin seemed the sort who never paid any heed to what anyone else thought of him.

Helen shook her head. Somehow, she couldn't seem to get a proper handle on the tall Frenchman and, between scouring through her wardrobe, and remembering their kiss, fifteen minutes had flown by. If she was honest with herself, she'd admit to being secretly thrilled to be having dinner with such an attractive man. Especially one who made her seem so desirable, regardless of her profession. A man who wasn't intimidated by her. It was a unique experience, even heady.

She finally decided on a twenties style flapper dress, one of three evening dresses she had brought with her. It was a simple sheath of peacock blue that ended above her knees, embellished with rows of beaded strands over the body and topped by spaghetti straps. She laughed when she pulled it out of the closet. It looked so dainty. But the hem didn't restrict her movement if she needed to run or kick someone. And the dress came with a matching narrow shawl that could, in a pinch, be used to strangle or trap an attacker. If only Yves knew what he was up against!

With the decision made, Helen had a quick shower in a bathroom that was as luxurious as she'd known it would be. The floor, counter and ledges were made of deep pink, polished marble against which the solid brass fittings gleamed. Fluffy white towels waited in a welcoming tower next to a timber bench, and there was every kind of toiletry Helen could possibly want, from body lotion to make-up remover.

Fluffing her hair, she dried it with the supplied hair-dryer then brushed it until it was silky and shiny. There was nothing she could do to completely tame her riotous locks, except restrain them with some heavy-duty clips, but she wasn't prepared to go that far. She wanted to enjoy the dinner, and relax for a change. With that in mind, she tucked her hair behind her ears and quickly did her make-up, giving her face a very light powder followed by strokes of blush, and accentuating her eyes with soft grey eyeliner. For lipstick, she used one of her stay-on peach-coloured standbys and added a thin film of clear gloss to give some shine.

Walking to the bedroom, she stepped into the dress, zipped it up, then stood back and performed a practice twirl in front of the full-length mirror. She might not be catwalk model material, but she didn't think she looked half bad. With a quick spray of perfume, she was done, and only just in time because a soft chime sounded through her suite. She grabbed her evening bag and slipped into a pair of dark strappy sandals, pulling at them with her fingers until her feet were comfortable then opened the door...and took a deep breath.

Helen had already seen Yves in casual business clothes, and he looked handsome enough. But he was nothing short of drop-dead gorgeous now. The lines of his Italian suit fit him like a glove—it must have been made to measure—the unbuttoned jacket revealed a snow-white shirt underneath, and the trousers tapered down, following the long lines of his legs. What surprised Helen was that he had not gone for a totally formal look. Not only the jacket but the top button of his shirt was undone. He exuded danger, forbidden pleasures, an invitation to hell. An Yves, coolly formal and aloof in proper business fashion, was someone she could handle. But an Yves who looked like he was winding down from a day's work, relaxed and a bit ruffled, was lethal.

Suddenly, Helen wasn't sure that having dinner with this disturbingly sensual man was such a good idea after all.

"I don't know that we should do this," she said with a suddenly dry throat.

He quirked his lips. "I wasn't aware that we had done anything. Yet."

Just that one word was enough to send riotous, x-rated images tumbling through her mind. It didn't help that he kept watching her with a lazy, yet intense, gaze. She had to get hold of herself. And fast.

"I mean, going out to dinner. We'll be leaving Mr. Aubrac alone and, while the staff here are unbelievably efficient, I doubt any of them have much experience at protecting a guest."

"You think he may be attacked?"

"It's a possibility." She took a breath and stood straighter. "I think it would be better to either stay in this evening," and every other evening for that matter, "or invite Mr. Aubrac along with us."

"Where you can keep those beautiful tourmaline eyes of yours on him?"

"Exactly." She tried to ignore the explicit compliment in his question. She had to think of the job. She had to think of the money.

"And what if I told you Mr. Aubrac is quite content to dine by himself and stay indoors tonight? I believe he told me he had much reading to catch up on. The financial markets in Europe are still open at this time."

She pitied him, if that was the case—a young, attractive man forced to spend traditional relaxation time poring over dull reports and analyst briefings. Did his family feel neglected as a result of his work? Did he even have a family?

"Is Mr. Aubrac married?" she asked without thinking.

Yves' gaze sharpened immediately. "Why? Are you interested in taming him, cherie? I admit, he's a very wealthy man."

Helen flushed, indignant. "Of course not. I just felt sorry for him and for his family. How much time could they have with him if he works every hour of the day?"

"You can make time for those things if you're sufficiently disciplined," he replied and put a hand on her elbow, drawing her forward. "Come, our dinner reservation is waiting."

"But I don't—"

"All we have is a little time before chaos descends on us, Helen. Within a few days, news will no doubt spread that a European company is seeking a partnership with an Australian firm. And, when that happens, attention may well fall on our little party, and you may be forced to earn every euro of that paycheque we've given you, hmm? But until then, we're in a small universe of peace and anonymity. Don't you think we should take advantage of that?"

Peace and anonymity. The way he phrased it sounded so seductive. He knew her line of work, and it didn't seem to bother him in the slightest. In fact, on some level, she thought it excited him. And, beneath the words, was another conversation completely—a carnal promise of hours of pleasure. Could she, she wondered, forget what she was and just accept some time together with a man? Without wondering if she was scaring him off or stepping on his masculinity?

In two weeks he'll be gone, a small voice whispered inside her. Why not take the chance to just be a woman for a change?

Two weeks of pleasure. Was it too much to ask for, especially after the torment of the past few months? As long as she made sure her dalliance with the delicious Yves Nerin didn't interfere with guarding Guy Aubrac, Helen couldn't see the problem with grabbing what pleasure she could while it lasted.

She smiled at him and her eyes twinkled. "That sounds like a good plan."

* * * *

It really shouldn't have been that difficult.

In the past, Yves would have directed Guy to make a booking in a particular town or city for a particular time, and that would have been the end of it. His assistant knew his preferences well enough to know what restaurants he should approach, and which he should avoid. But, here in Australia…!

He didn't know the country well. He could have asked the staff at Heritage House, of course, but he had the strange desire to make the choice himself. So strange, he didn't even task Guy with the job, but instead trawled through both print and online street directories, searching for recommendations. He was used to eating late, but that was a distinctly continental thing. Australians and Americans preferred to eat earlier as a general rule, he knew. So, eight o'clock was too late, but was seven o'clock fine? By the time Yves factored in a couple of pre-dinner cocktails and some light conversation, they would end up eating at eight anyway, so did it make that much of a difference?

And what kind of food did she prefer? Would she think it too parochial if he chose a French restaurant? Or would he be better off with Australian cuisine? But perhaps, she wanted a change, in which case he was back to French again.

Finally, he decided on a restaurant that was part of a five-star hotel built on a hill on the outskirts of the city centre. The restaurant served international cuisine, which he thought would cater for all tastes, and was situated at the very top of the building, so it had magnificent views of the surrounding landscape. Hopefully, the twinkling night lights of the city would help calm his prickly little bodyguard.

Was that why he was taking such unusual, inordinate, care with the evening's arrangements? Was it because of the vulnerability she tried so very hard to hide, but which peeked out from under those long, smoky lashes at him? Or was it the novelty of meeting a woman who didn't go around asking for help in every situation? Yves thought back to his previous mistresses — most of them thought he liked it if they pretended to be helpless about everything and, up till this moment, he thought he liked it, too. It came naturally to him to help out a female companion with choosing a new car or a new wardrobe. Truth be told, it gave his ego a boost to be fawned over and listened to by so many women. But now that he met this feisty, blonde Australian, he wondered if he was selling himself and his previous companions short. Instead of a lift to his ego, he felt an undeserved stab of pride when he thought back to his encounter with Helen in the meeting room. She was efficient and professional, yet she was also courteous and warm. And it didn't hurt that she had a dynamite body, toned muscles under smooth creamy skin, and long legs that he ached to have wrapped around his own hips.

She was sparkling and humorous and intelligent. And exactly what he needed.

What he wanted in a woman, he realised with a jolt, was not a sycophant but an equal. Was Helen Collier such a woman? He pondered the thought right up 'til the moment he rang the bell on her suite.

If he thought her legs were slim and long in the trousers she had worn earlier in the day, they seemed to go on forever in the number she greeted him with. The strappy dress looked wonderful on her, the beads shimmering with each movement she made. With a matching shawl slung casually around her neck, and a mischievous look in her eyes, she was everything he could have wished for, and he was glad he had taken the initiative that afternoon and more or less ordered her to dinner with him. But the longer he looked at her, the more reluctant he was to go out in public. Instead, he wanted to lead her back into her suite and spend the night exploring every inch of that taut, toned body, to lose himself in her honeyed curls. And that unnerved him. Yves considered his self-control to be one of his most formidable traits. To realise that a pair of blue-grey eyes were enough to undermine it was not a comfortable thought. With a little more abruptness than was necessary, he sketched Helen a brief nod and ushered her to the front door.

The private car was waiting, as expected, when they stepped out of Heritage House, and they travelled in plush, air-conditioned comfort to the hotel's grand portico. Yves was a bit more relaxed when they arrived, and he helped her out with a courteous hand, feeling a little smug—truth be known—at the masculine glances that were cast his way. Helen was too much woman for any of them to handle, he thought to himself. Any of them…but him.

He had never visited the restaurant before, but the staff were deferential. He asked Helen if she would prefer an aperitif before dinner and was happy when she agreed. With a quiet word to the maitre'd, they moved to the long bar, picking two high bar-chairs at one end to give them a degree of privacy.

"You know," she murmured, "I've lived in Brisbane all my life, yet I've never been in this restaurant."

"Does it meet with your approval?" he asked casually.

"Oh yes. The view from here is breathtaking."

That is not the only thing that is, he thought to himself. When the bartender sidled over with their drinks—a dry sherry for her, and a vodka martini for him—Yves deliberately leant over a little farther than necessary when placing the slender glass close to her, taking a deep breath of her hair and skin as he did so. She smelt of lemons and flowers and an underlying musk that told him she was as captured by him as he was with her. The problems of Leonid Alexandrov and the interrupted matters he left behind in France faded into the distance.

"That's Mt. Coot-tha," she told him, pointing out a peak, dark but for a smattering of lights at its crown. "It's the tallest point in Brisbane."

"Do people live on its summit?" he asked, not so much because he was interested in her answer, but just to hear the energy and enthusiasm in her voice.

"Oh no," she laughed. "Not right at the top. There's a lookout there and a nice restaurant. The views are quite spectacular."

"Perhaps we could go there sometime this week?" He watched her animated profile, letting a promise of illicit pleasure light his eyes as he willed her to turn to him.

"Yes." She swung towards him and shuddered to a halt as she stared him full in the face. Suddenly, those eyes of hers were huge, dark with pupils that were almost fully dilated. He heard a breath catch in her throat, and saw the answer written plainly on her face, even if she didn't know it herself.

Bien. It took immense will power to casually reach for his glass and take a sip of his astringent drink.

"I'd like that very much," he said, slipping back into his role of agreeable visitor. "To see a bit of this city before I go back to France."

Her eyes narrowed and Yves saw the woman of the previous moment disappear, to be replaced by the professional. "Oh. Isn't Mr. Aubrac going back with you?"

Merde! He kept on tripping himself up with this childish subterfuge of his, which was not a clever thing to do in front of a woman who was keeping him on his toes so successfully.

"Of course I'm hoping Mr. Aubrac and I will be returning together," he told her smoothly. "But it's not uncommon for a sudden matter to crop up that demands his urgent attention." He drained his drink and got to his feet, noticing that she had barely touched her sherry. "Come, let us have some dinner. I'll ask the waiter to bring your glass to the table."

The main dining area was further along the huge tinted glass wall, and they were shown to a table with a lovely view of the city and provided with menus and a wine list.

"What's it like in France?" she asked, looking over at him. "Do you live in Paris?"

"I have houses in Paris, Nice, Cannes and Grenoble," he replied easily, scanning the menu.

"Really?"

He knew what she was thinking just by the tone of her voice. She was wondering how an assistant — albeit an assistant to a very wealthy man — could afford so many properties. Once more he had put his giant foot straight into it.

"Well, Mr. Aubrac owns them," he added quickly. "But he lets me use them when I'm vacationing."

"I see." But she still looked sceptical.

"Do you see anything you like?" he asked, indicating the menu with his hand. He hoped to distract her with the question and, thankfully, it worked. She looked down and shook her head with a small laugh.

"It all sounds so good. I'm not sure what to choose."

"Choose whatever you would normally not eat," he told her, watching her face. "Think of tonight as a special evening."

She smiled happily at that, the curve slowly forming on her lips, and he sat back, content. This was what having dinner with a beautiful woman was all about. Charm, grace, the ability to provide the other person with something out of the ordinary, whether it was a meal at an expensive restaurant, or coaxing a tender smile from a reluctant woman. She bent her head to look again at the menu and they passed the minutes in companionable silence.

Yves surreptitiously scanned the restaurant when he was done making his choices. This was a much quieter place than what he was normally used to. Back in Europe, friends and business acquaintances often interrupted his dining out, strolling over with casual greetings, or sending a bottle of something—usually vintage and sparkling—to his table. And, up till now, he had enjoyed the banter and nods of acknowledgement that flashed across crowded rooms of people. But here was a different world. The tables were further apart, the room less filled, and he didn't recognise any other person in the world. Maybe it was also subconscious relief from being away from Alexandrov's pernicious presence, but Yves couldn't ever remember feeling so relaxed before and so appreciative of his privacy.

The waiter came over to get their order, and Yves resented even this interruption. For tonight, he wanted Helen all to himself.

"Bodyguard duties are unusual for a woman," he commented, after they had ordered and the waiter discreetly slipped away.

As if on cue, he saw the prickles come out again.

"I'm just making an observation," he added, attempting to mollify her. It worked, to a degree. The sharp spikes retracted somewhat, but Yves thought he could still see their metaphoric points glinting in the subdued restaurant lighting.

She smiled wryly. "You're right. I suppose I'm being a little sensitive."

"What made you go into such a line of work?"

"It's actually a sideline," she admitted candidly. That was something else he liked about her — her open and refreshing honesty. A marked contrast to you, eh Yves, a sly part of him commented, but he brushed the thought aside. He had reasons for what he did, and valid ones at that. It didn't compare.

"I began training in martial arts more as something to do. I heard Ryan Greenwood was the best, so I became one of his students. Later, I graduated to instructor. And then I saw an opportunity to do some good with it."

"Such as?" he prompted.

"Conducting workshops and seminars for women who want to learn how to protect themselves. I've also held series of classes for various companies in Queensland. The owners usually tell me they see positive results from such courses — more energy, more self-esteem — and I get the opportunity to boost people's interests, get them interested in something physical, and improve their self-confidence."

"So you're not usually a bodyguard?" Why did he ever think she was only just one thing? Her quick mind was enough to show him that there were many facets to Helen Collier.

"It's nice work," she said hurriedly. "But it's like icing on the cake, really. Like my private students."

"You give one-on-one instruction?"

"Of course. It can be tiring, but it's also rewarding being able to focus on just one person."

"Just women?" He tried to sound casual, but there must have been something — just the hint of bite — in his voice, because she looked at him sharply.

"No, not necessarily. I have both male and female private students."

"Indeed. How interesting."

But, inside, Yves' gut clenched. He imagined those slim, enticing curves as close to someone else as they'd been to him—alors, was it only this morning? Was she like that with her male students, stepping through a physical dance almost as intimate as sex? He remembered her distinctly keeping close to him as he fell to the floor, her face sometimes mere inches from his. He thought of her highly-tuned sense of awareness in being able to do this, and wanted that awareness, that strength, in bed with him—above him, below him, holding and squeezing. Yves imagined touching her smooth skin, encouraging those strong fingers to dig into his flesh, feeling those sleek muscles tense as she threw her head back and yelled for release.

And, just then, their first course arrived. Yves unclenched the death grip he held on the napkin in his lap, and smiled politely at Helen, across the table.

"Oh, I don't think I should drink anything," she protested, when the sommelier approached them with the bottle of Chablis he had ordered.

"I thought we agreed. One evening of peace, before the real work begins."

He saw the wavering doubt in her mind and was pleased when she gave in. He knew it was because of him. Because she wanted to let down her guard with him. It was good to know that this fever that gripped him was mutual.

Later, Yves could have described few things about their meal—that the foie gras was a little overcooked for his liking, but the seafood main course was superb. The hours sped away in a way they never had before. He and Helen spoke on a range of issues, from running businesses to history snippets about Australia. He surprised himself by telling her a little about Grenoble and what he liked about that small plateau city, high in the mountains, and was impressed by how much she wanted to learn about everything that touched on his life. They laughed and talked through dessert then through a liqueur with coffee, and it was almost midnight when they finally paused and noticed they were the only couple left in the restaurant.

Yves felt like a teenager again as a quick laugh escaped his lips. He had noticed little else but the lively young woman in front of him. Grabbing Helen by the hand, he paid their bill and they left, catching a taxi from the front of the hotel for the brief ride back to Heritage House.

Their good cheer left them suddenly at the door to her suite. One minute, they were smiling, and walking together with good-natured ease. The next, a thick tension descended upon them. Yves gazed down into Helen's blue-grey eyes, and the breath caught in his throat. It was like he was drowning in a lagoon of clear water, unable to tell exactly how deeply under he was. And not caring.

With rough hands, he hauled her up hard to his body. That he caught her by surprise was good. She was in the middle of a startled gasp, and he took advantage of it by capturing her lips with his. He didn't tease or tantalise but made sure she knew exactly what he was thinking, what he was fantasising. He sought out her tongue in the soft, moist interior of her mouth, flicking at it, promising pleasure, letting her know that he was well-versed in the curves and hollows of a woman's body and that she would be safe in his arms.

He pulled away momentarily, to nip gently at her lower lip then nuzzle her neck, breathing in the fresh, floral scent of her, then kissed her again. He felt the momentary hesitation in her movements—he swore he could feel her heart beating next to his—then her hands moved upwards, clutching his hair and deepening the embrace.

She was so warm, so welcoming, and Yves felt himself harden. They were so close, he knew she couldn't help but feel his arousal against her hips. His left hand travelled down her body, over her waist and the rows of rough beads. When he reached the hem, he hitched his hand underneath, and stroked upwards, her skin smooth and sensuous after the texture of her dress. He cupped her backside and pulled her closer, and she moaned silently into his mouth, swaying her hips so they pressed against him in a primal rhythm.

"We should go inside your suite," he whispered hoarsely after reluctantly releasing her lips. He looked down and was gratified by the stunned, dark arousal in her eyes and the swollen plumpness of her lips. He savoured the look on her face. Dieu, if this is how she looked now, already flushed and wanton, how would she look after a night of love-making? His body, his groin, his mouth, ached to find out.

"I..." She looked up at him, dazed.

She didn't have to say a word, he could read it in her eyes. We shouldn't be doing this. We both have our jobs to do. This is unprofessional.

Yves didn't give a damn. And he was going to make sure Helen didn't either. Without giving her time to say one word more, he swung her into his arms and elbowed his way into her suite.

They didn't make it to the bedroom. The living room was lit by one soft lamp, throwing the furniture into sumptuous and enticing relief, and Yves was too impatient to disregard the sudden images that filled his head. Putting Helen on her feet, he kissed her while throwing off his clothes. His jacket and shirt fell into an untidy heap on the floor. Shucking his shoes, he kicked the pile out of the way, his lips still locked on Helen's. They parted, reluctantly, while she unzipped her dress and lifted it over her head, revealing an expanse of smooth, creamy skin.

"I don't think we need this," Yves murmured, unhooking her bra and gently pulling the clear, thin straps down her arms. It went the same way as his clothes. His hands replaced the lingerie, cupping her breasts and running his thumbs over the soft flesh.

"Exquisite." He pulled her against his chest and slid his hands around to her back, following the graceful contour of her body down to her panties. Even the conservative cut of her underwear couldn't stop the blaze of desire that enveloped him. As he pushed his hips against her groin, one hand grabbed at the stretchy material, gently pulling on it. The pressure made her panties contract, falling into the crack between her legs, throwing her backside into bare relief. Slowly, Yves followed the line made by the lingerie, a finger boldly pressing against her. It moved further, until he felt moisture against his fingertips. Flicking the flimsy cotton to one side, he pushed his finger into her as she moaned against his chest.

"You like that?" he asked softly.

"Yes," was the muffled response.

He withdrew his finger and dragged her down to the carpeted floor, pushing her so her back rested against the plump leather of the sofa. Her head was thrown back, her eyes closed in anticipation of ecstasy. Her legs, still encased in her strappy shoes, splayed open in front of him.

Yves quickly discarded the rest of his clothing, letting his erection bob freely against his abdomen. He felt coiled and leashed inside with an urge to bury himself in Helen, but he resisted. Pinning her arms to the sofa, he bent down between her legs and licked at her pussy through her panties. The texture was of soft-thick cotton, but salty and arousing with Helen's own juices. She bucked against him. Using his teeth, he moved the elastic to one side, and thrust his tongue inside her, sucking on her wetness before flicking her erect clitoris. Helen moaned loudly and spread her legs even further apart, the dim light highlighting the line of her thigh muscles as she exposed herself to him.

He wanted to take it easy, wanted to stretch out the time and pleasure he was giving and receiving, but the sight of Helen, and the scent of her, drove him wild. Moving quickly, he positioned himself over her, bending to rub his face against her cheek so she could smell herself on him. She tried to say something, but her voice was thick and inarticulate. He paused only long enough to retrieve and rip open a small packet from his trouser pocket, sheathing himself then, using his hand, he guided himself into her, groaning at the hot, tight sensation that gripped his cock and massaged his length as he moved in and out, preparing herself for him before he drove into her fully.

The fact that she wanted him, that she was so slick and wet already, made him harder. He increased the tempo, feeling her clench against him while her hands fluttered beneath his grip. Stretched wide, she gave herself to him, her breathing loud and hurried in the room, a higher counterpoint to his own rasps of pleasure. Yves thought of her, her feet arched and bound with thin leather straps, her wrists imprisoned by his fingers, her breasts and sex rubbing against him. She was moving now, her legs and body restless, her arms straining against him, as the first throes of orgasm took over her body. Yves increased his own tempo, watching her as the climax built in his own body, radiating out from his cock and making him clench his buttocks. Her lips glistened, her face was flushed. She opened startled eyes, almost black and unseeing, as the climax broke over her. Her spasms squeezed his already-sensitive organ, and he slammed into her, caught up in the waves, pouring himself into her as he shouted his release out loud. They remained slaves to convulsions out of their control, each trying to spin out the moment for as long as possible before they collapsed to the carpet together, breathing heavily and unable to speak for many minutes.

Chapter Five

Helen woke with an aching body and a feeling of uncommon lassitude. Startled, she looked over to the other side of the bed, but it was empty. Remembering what had happened last night, she groaned and flopped back onto the pillow.

"How could I have been so stupid?" she muttered. As if once hadn't been enough, she and Yves had managed to make it to the bedroom for their second time. And third. It embarrassed the hell out of Helen just remembering what they had done to each other's bodies. Wantonly, she licked her lips, but the pressure of his cock in her mouth was long gone.

Slowly, as if she was an old woman, she rose and walked to the bathroom. Her sex ached from the exercise she had put it through the previous night. She should feel sated, yet all she wanted to do was tumble into bed with Yves again and repeat every single thing they had done together the night before. If Helen didn't know better, she'd think she was fast becoming addicted to Yves. That didn't bode well for the next two weeks.

It seemed Yves had made a deliberate effort to set her at her ease at the dinner, being a charming and teasing conversationalist. The food had matched the mood—delicious and enjoyable—and everything had gone well, courteous and above board, she thought...until they got to the door of her suite.

Helen thought back to those moments and to the erotic adventure that had followed. She knew she didn't have anyone else to blame for the impulse that had overtaken her. She'd wanted to kiss Yves and be kissed by him. She'd wanted to know what it felt like to be held by him, stroked by him. She'd wanted to throw all caution to the wind, lead him to the bedroom, discarding clothes as they went, and lose herself with him through all the hours of darkness. And she had. But in the cold light of day, her actions seemed nothing short of criminally irresponsible.

For a start, he was associated with her client—a client Ryan had passed along to her because she needed the money. Getting involved with Yves Nerin would not only let down Guy Aubrac but could also damage Ryan's reputation internationally. She couldn't do that to someone she regarded as a friend and mentor.

And there was Pete. Ryan had known about their tentative plans for the future, even though he kept his tone light and impersonal. Having trained both people, he'd watched them with an eagle eye of a senior instructor. How could he not have known that Helen and Pete had contemplated establishing themselves as a couple?

Helen sank onto the bed with her shirt half undone and groaned.

It didn't make any sense. She and Pete had been perfectly suited. Helen wouldn't have called it the passion of her life but, in her line of work, there was no such thing. With men who were either too intimidated by her, or used her and her profession as a way of proving their masculinity, she had long ago resigned herself to nothing more than a comfortable relationship, at best. And Pete had been comfortable. Being a fellow instructor, he hadn't been scared of her or felt the need to dominate their fledgling romance. He'd never charged to the rescue, had been confident that Helen could sort out whatever situation she found herself in, and had understood the lack of consistency in her schedule. She'd never had to bother explaining herself to him in situations where she had to urgently backfill an evening class of eager students. Pete had understood her. That was what made this blazing attraction she felt for the Frenchman all the more difficult—Pete had been so understanding. And now he was dead and buried, and she was jumping in the sack with the arrogant assistant of her first high-powered, international client.

She remembered the feel of Yves' body against hers. This man wasn't as patient as Pete had been. She could imagine Yves fighting through a crowd to reach the woman he loved, never mind that she might be capable of looking after herself. He would just consider it his duty to be there, helping protect her. Maybe that was part of what was so seductive about Yves Nerin, the knowledge that there was a support there for her if she ever needed it.

If she ever held Yves' interest. If he ever fell in love with someone like her.

If.

And here she was, creating fantasies out of thin air. In less than two weeks—two weeks!?both men would be out of her life, and she would be left to pick up pieces from her encounter with them, in addition to the guilt she felt over her betrayal of Pete's memory.

Somehow, she had to forget what had happened the night before and resist Yves Nerin, even if it was the hardest thing she had ever done in her life. She had to live up to Ryan's opinion of her, respect the memory of the man she had thought to share her life with, and forget a burning pair of blue eyes, long hard body and deliciously stimulating cock.

The first way to achieve that was to not ever be alone with him again, let alone be seduced into something that appeared innocuous, such as another invitation to dinner. The second was to firmly put her emotions somewhere in deep freeze and think of Pete. And the third was to remember how much she was going to earn from this assignment and how much she had to lose if she messed up in any way.

Helen switched on the water in the shower cubicle and stepped inside, sluicing her body with the cool spray. That was better. She definitely felt more in control now.

By the time she exited her suite, she thought she had regained control. As she walked along the passage, a member of the Heritage House staff told her that breakfast was being served outside on the lawn. With a smile, Helen continued through the foyer and let herself out through the large French doors.

It was a beautiful morning. Being October, the bite of summer had not yet begun, but the air was warm and filled with the sounds of passing ferries and the muted buzz of morning commuter traffic from the Pacific Motorway set high above the Brisbane River.

She felt comfortable in her clothes, a pair of khaki capri pants, short-sleeved, white, tailored cotton shirt and sneakers. She knew the outfit made her look like a college student, but it was good for movement, and it blended in well with Brisbane pedestrians. The gentlemen, she was happy to see, had obviously come to the same conclusion as she had. Guy was already seated at the circular black wrought-iron table and was wearing a peach-coloured polo shirt and brown chinos. Yves — she faltered for a second when she saw him, before stiffening her spine and continuing as if nothing was amiss — was still serving himself from a long table of breakfast items set buffet-style against the house wall. Even when in casual clothes, he was still a handful and a half of man, and Helen tried very hard not to notice the way the blue-striped polo shirt he wore stretched across his chest, outlining the tantalising lines of his pectorals or the way the lighter casual pants hugged his thighs. The man would stand out no matter where he was, whether it was in the middle of a Moroccan marketplace or an Australian shopping plaza. Her eyes moved once more down to his bare left hand. It seemed strange that he was still unattached. Unless, she paused as the thought suddenly hit her, he was one of those 'modern' men who didn't wear a wedding ring. That made it triply important to stay away from him. As if she needed yet another ironclad reason.

Yves looked up as she approached the table. She flashed him a sunny but otherwise impersonal smile —

well aware of her seated employer—and took a plate from the stack at one end of the breakfast spread.

"Lovely morning, isn't it?" she asked brightly then looked away, concentrating hard on a dish of scrambled eggs kept warm by a small burner beneath it.

"It is now," he replied quietly, moving up close to her, an empty plate in his own hand.

Helen pretended not to hear. Or notice.

"Did you sleep well?" he continued. It was an innocent enough question, but she heard the small thread of laughter beneath it and clutched the serving spoon tighter.

"Very." She treated the eggs abominably as she slapped a dollop onto her plate and quickly moved on, avoiding the bacon and sausages for the plain reason that he was right next to them.

Unfortunately, he caught up with her at the toaster, where she had thoughtlessly popped in two slices and was thus forced to wait for their re-emergence.

"What about you?" she asked sweetly, looking up at him, determined to not give him the entire upper hand.

That was a mistake. His eyes glinted merrily under the warm sun and she wanted to melt into her sneakers. Even looking at him was a dangerous pastime. She averted her eyes and cursed the bread for taking such a long time.

"I slept very peacefully," he said urbanely.

The toast finally popped, and Helen swept them onto her plate with haste. It was only as she walked away that she heard him add, "Eventually."

Her step almost faltered again, but she steadied herself. Pinning another smile on her face, Helen approached the circular table. "Good morning, Mr. Aubrac."

Guy smiled but it wasn't as lethally edged as the one that belonged to Yves. Helen felt herself relax as she sat down.

"Good morning, Helen." He pronounced her name the French way, dropping the initial letter. "Did you have a good sleep?"

What was it with people obsessed with her slumber, she thought.

"Yes I did, thank you." She buttered her toast and took a bite. "May I ask what you're planning for today?"

"We have arranged our first meeting with Tech-88 for tomorrow morning. But, as preparation, Yves, er, suggested that we should perhaps take a walk around the suburb where they're situated. We very much believe in getting a feel for our business partners before we begin formal negotiations."

"I see. May I ask where the company is located?"

"New Farm," Yves interposed smoothly, slipping into the chair next to hers. Unlike her appetite, which had fled the moment she caught sight of him, his plate was piled high with food. "Do you know it?"

"Know it?" Helen laughed. "It's one of the oldest suburbs in Brisbane. And a lovely place."

"Is it very far from here?"

She shook her head. "Not at all. We can finish breakfast, let the morning traffic settle down, and be on our way."

"I have ordered a taxi for ten thirty," Yves said. "Will that give us sufficient time to get there?"

"We can be there, have a walk around, and still have plenty of time for lunch."

"D'accord. Then it's settled."

Helen didn't taste the rest of her breakfast. She couldn't tell if the eggs were light and fluffy or resembled half-set cement. All she was aware of was Yves' thigh close to hers, and the woodsy scent of his aftershave that drifted across to her nostrils, teasing her with memories of intimacy. What would it be like to wake up to that fragrance, she wondered. To breathe that in when she first opened her eyes in the morning, knowing exactly who it was lying in bed next to her, an arm perhaps carelessly thrown across her body, their legs entwined.

Her breakfast turned to ashes in her mouth, and she pushed the plate away, her food only half-eaten. Of course, Yves noticed. Helen knew enough by now to know nothing much missed that razor-sharp gaze. But he only lifted an eyebrow in curiosity and said nothing.

After a brief discussion on the company they were going to see over their last cups of coffee, Helen grabbed her sling bag, and they headed for New Farm. The taxi passed the street where Helen lived, and she couldn't resist a quick look down the narrow avenue, although she wasn't exactly sure what she was expecting. Was it really only two days since she'd met Ryan and been offered the bodyguard assignment?

"Is something the matter?" Yves asked softly. Guy was sitting in front, leaving her and Yves in the back. Once more, he had managed to outmanoeuvre her.

"I...live down there," she finally said. She didn't want to tell him that information, didn't want to give him any other insight into her own life, but it would have been rude to ignore him as he was a client of hers.

To her relief, he nodded but said nothing.

The taxi swung in a block-long u-turn and continued on its way. Helen watched as the commercial district of Fortitude Valley gave way to the small houses and cheerful gardens of New Farm. As the car continued further into the suburb, the trees along the footpaths grew taller, and wide side-streets provided glimpses of stately houses on high stilts, shaded by fig trees and just-blooming jacaranda trees.

One of her friends, Sue Thompson, lived in the suburb, running her graphic design business from her house. Sue had often implored her to move to the greener location, but Helen had always refused. She liked the air of dynamism associated with the revived commercial locality. New Farm, on the other hand, was a lot quieter here than in the lively Valley—a characteristic that Helen felt had no appeal, until now.

"It's very nice," Guy commented from the front.

"We'll stop by the park," Helen said, "and I'll take you for a walk around. You'll be able to see where the company has its business, and we can stop for a coffee if you'd like."

She should be in the front seat, she knew that much. That would give her the best view of what was happening around the car, and it would get her away from the tempting presence of Yves. She would not allow herself to be manipulated again.

The taxi driver let them out with a smile, right next to one of the largest parks in the city, and Helen took a deep breath as she looked around.

"This used to be farming country," she explained to the men, orienting them. "If you continue walking down there, you'll get to the river again."

"These houses are very pretty," Guy commented. "The woodwork on some is quite—how do you say it?—ornate."

"A lot of the houses here have been renovated. This whole suburb was not a very nice place to live for a couple of decades. There was a lot of crime around. Then people discovered how close it was to the city, and money started pouring in. Families moved here, bought houses and renovated them."

They strolled by the edge of the park, watching playgroups shout and scamper over the swings, ladders and other equipment arranged in open circles. Further along, small children played among the trees. In one marked out rectangle, a man who was obviously a coach took a group of young students through the basics of soccer. A few elderly people watched the budding athletes from a shady bench.

"New Farm has always been home to a variety of cultures," she continued, "and that hasn't changed. And the bakeries here are fabulous." She slanted a mischievous look at Yves from under her lashes. "You might even find bread that reminds you of home."

He smiled and the day suddenly appeared brighter. "I shall make it a point to look."

KS Augustin

"Down here," she indicated a broad avenue off the main street, "is where Tech-88 is located, from the information you gave me. They operate out of their own low-rise building."

"Is that usual?" Guy asked. "For companies in Australia to operate out of residential areas?"

Helen pursed her lips. "It depends. A lot of small businesses operate out of the owners' homes." She thought of Sue and how well the arrangement worked for her. "For larger companies, it's a little unusual to be situated out of the city centre but not too much. After all, it's noisy and expensive in the city. Maybe the owners of Tech-88 thought their employees would appreciate a nicer environment."

Yves looked around. "Cheaper parking, I presume. Nicer surroundings. Lower rent?" He looked at Helen, who shrugged apologetically. He took that as agreement. "More relaxed atmosphere. Guy," he launched into a quick string of sentences in French then turned to her. "I was just telling my, er, employer that the owners of the company seem to be good thinkers. I still have some questions regarding their choice of location, but I'm sure that will be answered when we meet with them tomorrow morning."

"We can take a walk around then stop for a coffee," Helen suggested.

Guy shrugged. "Yes, why not?"

The three of them continued to skirt the park.

This would have to be one of the easiest assignments she had been on, Helen thought. Her jobs with Ryan were usually of a higher profile, such as escorting Japanese businessmen to the casinos and making sure they were not spied on by the criminal element. In one memorable assignment, they had even escorted a nervous African head of state to the Gold Coast so he could purchase some beachfront property for one of his mistresses. Helen still smiled when she thought of that one. The man was tall, obviously rich, and good looking — despite his obvious apprehension — but that hadn't stopped him propositioning Helen himself. She politely and firmly refused. She had often been the target of some light-hearted flirting from her clients, and she had been impervious to their charms. But, somehow, Yves had managed to effortlessly find a way beneath that. That made Helen uneasy.

They finally stopped at an outdoor cafe across the road, along a strip of small shops. The wonderful fragrance of freshly-baked bread wafted across to them from the bakery next door as they seated themselves at a small table. Helen made sure to take the chair that afforded her the best view of the street and who was walking in and out of the cafe.

"Is the weather here always so lovely?" Guy asked, as they waited for their coffees.

"I think so." She smiled. "But, then again, considering I'm a Queenslander, born and bred, I could be biased."

She also wondered what kind of job paid as well as it did, merely so she could sit in the sun and enjoy a latte. She was still a bit surprised by Guy's request for a bodyguard. Who would dare attack two businessmen attempting to negotiate a software partnership deal? It didn't make sense. And what would she have done with the money if Pete had still been around? Maybe she would have suggested an expensive holiday for the both of them, to explore whether there was any promise in the tickle of attraction they'd felt towards each other.

A tickle that had been drowned by a soul-shaking earthquake when she met Yves Nerin. The realisation made her feel guilty…and cheap.

"I think we should start heading back," Yves suggested as they drained the last of their drinks. "Mr. Aubrac and I will need to discuss how we approach our first meeting with Tech-88. Just the walk around has given me much to think upon. Thank you for your company, Helen."

Hey, it's my job, she wanted to say, but knew he was just being gracious, maybe even trying to set her mind at ease after the tumult of the night before. She smiled. "I'm happy you found it so helpful."

Just as they rose, Helen heard her name being called, and turned in the direction of the bakery, her face lighting with delight when she saw who it was who caught her attention.

"Gentlemen," she said, "could you excuse me for a few moments? There's someone I need to have a brief word with."

At their relaxed nods, she rose and walked over to a young woman, dressed in a T-shirt and jogging pants, holding a paper bag. From out of the opening, Helen saw the rounded end of one of the bakery's famous olive bread concoctions. Sue Thompson was a bright, bubbly and creative graphic artist who lived in the suburb. Her chestnut hair was pulled back in ponytail, and her hazel eyes glinted merrily as she watched Helen approach.

"Hey you," she greeted casually. "Where have you been? I've been trying to get you on the phone for the past couple of days."

Helen angled herself so she could still keep an eye on her two charges. "Sorry, I haven't been home for a while. Work," she explained.

"With those two hunks at the table with you? Some work." Sue snorted. "Was this a job from Ryan? Guarding some boring nation's royal jewels or artwork? Or guarding them while they drop millions at the roulette table?" She knew about Helen's professional relationship with her old instructor and liked to tease her about the kind of bodyguard jobs she occasionally took on.

Helen grinned. "Something like that."

"Some people have all the luck. Meanwhile, I have to sit down and think of a creative ad for a pet shampoo business."

Helen listened to her friend with half an ear, her eyes alert as she scanned the slowly milling crowd along the shopping strip. Then she saw it, and her heart dropped.

It was just her luck that she was only congratulating herself on catching such a lucrative contract a few minutes before, and here was trouble walking, as brazen as brass, towards her.

Not that either of the young men knew she was in any way associated with either Guy or Yves. They were both tall and lean, dressed casually in T-shirts and jeans, and everybody's eyes would have sidled straight past them. But not Helen's. They weren't walking the walk of casual visitors to one of the most popular spots in Brisbane. They were specifically looking for something or someone. And from the way they jerked still for a second when they spotted the Frenchmen, then exchanged hurried whispers before circling away, Helen knew that these two were one of the reasons why she had landed the contract. Strange how she had never thought of computer software before as being such a dangerous business.

"...Saint Nerin," Sue was saying excitedly.

Helen snapped back to the tail-end of her friend's sentence. "What did you say?"

She still watched the two men as they loitered by the corner. Helen glanced away from them, further up the mall, sizing up her chances.

"You never listen to anything I say," Sue complained good-naturedly. "I said, you lead such an isolated life, I wouldn't be surprised if you hadn't recognised the great de Saint Nerin himself."

"The great...," Helen paused, obviously puzzled, and Sue rolled her eyes.

"You really don't know, do you? He's only France's hottest property, in more ways that one. Money pouring out of his ears. Of Russian parentage, from what I've read, hence his name."

"Saint Nerin?" Why did Helen feel like she was suddenly floundering in quicksand?

"No, silly. Yvegeny. His name is Yvegeny de Saint Nerin."

A terrible realisation dawned on Helen. Yvegeny? Shortened to — Yves? And Saint Nerin reduced to Nerin? "What about Guy Aubrac?" she asked faintly, still watching the two young men.

Sue shrugged. "Don't know that name. But Saint Nerin is the one to watch out for. He has businesses all over Europe, holiday homes all over the place, too. Not married, but he goes through the women like a hot knife through soft butter."

I have houses in Paris, Nice, Cannes and Grenoble.

Helen remembered his words over dinner. He'd tried to cover the slip and make it appear that he only borrowed Guy's houses from time to time, but Helen now knew it for the lie it was. How stupid of her that she hadn't realised it earlier. Guy Aubrac wasn't the wealthy one, it was Yves—sorry, Yvegeny—with his air of authority and crisp intelligence who owned the millions. Yves was the owner, and it was Guy who was his assistant. It was all so clear now.

Helen's anger simmered. Which made their little dinner and tryst together...what? Slumming it with one of the natives?

The two young men at the corner made a gesture of impatience, and Helen cut her friend short. "I've got to go, Sue. I'll give you a call. Soon."

She thought furiously as she strolled back to the men, deliberately ignoring the two at the corner of the shop. Heading back that way was out of the question. She didn't want to walk further along the strip either; the young men would follow them. Maybe they could avoid a confrontation altogether? Helen looked across the road but, just then, a group of uniformed children arrived, obviously on their way back to school after a play in the park.

"I think it would be better if we walked further along the shops," she said with a smile, but Yves picked up on the note of strain in her voice.

"Is something the matter?" he asked, his gaze boring into hers.

"Maybe."

To their credit, both men took the news in stride, rising easily from their chairs and even chatting as they walked away. Helen laughed at an opportune moment, and tracked the other two in the reflection of the shops' plate glass windows. Not only were they following, but they were gaining on them.

There was no time to call the police—they would arrive too late to be any good—and no empty taxis nearby to conveniently slip into. Helen hated having to resort to this, always preferring to pre-emptively move out of danger rather than having to confront it directly, but she had no choice. Seeing a side passage between two shops, she directed the men down there.

When their would-be attackers followed, Helen was ready.

She had already moved back to position at the foot of the passage, and as the first youth hurried around the corner, a grin of anticipation still on his face, she punched him, low and hard, in the gut, before throwing him against a wall. The second one, now warned, tried to rush her, but a check kick to his knee stopped him. Helen struck him a few times—body and head—and bent low enough to spin and deliver an uppercut to the first man, who had recovered from the throw. Both attackers hit the ground almost at the same time.

"I've got to call the police," Helen said hurriedly, pulling her mobile out of her back pocket, but an iron grasp on her wrist stopped her.

"Non!"

She looked into the deep blue of Yves' eyes with disbelief. "I've got to call the police," she repeated.

"Non. We will leave." One of the men on the ground started groaning. "I shall explain when we get home."

"You bet you will," Helen conceded bitterly, putting her phone away with one brutal movement. "And I'm looking forward to your story, Monsieur de Saint Nerin."

Chapter Six

It took forty minutes, which was forty minutes longer than she liked, before they were back in the meeting room where Helen's interview had originally been conducted. Yves had insisted that she take a shower and change before they even discussed what had happened, something she was reluctantly grateful for, and there was already hot tea, coffee and a plate of sandwiches waiting for her when she entered. She was too incensed to care that her hair was still damp or that there were spots of bright red on her scrubbed cheeks. She hated being played for a fool, and that was something Yves had managed to do within minutes of meeting her.

"Are you hurt?" he asked first, rising quickly and moving towards her. He reached for her hands and inspected her knuckles, but there were no bruises on her fair skin, just a redness along the back of her right hand that would disappear soon.

Helen snatched back her hands and seated herself with a mutinous purse of her lips. "I'm fine. Why didn't you let me call the police?"

"You know who I am," he remarked, ignoring the question. "I presume the friend you met near the cafe told you."

"Yes, indeed." There was a slight hiss to her answer. "She was only too happy to inform me that my 'client' is actually my client's secretary." She looked at Guy in enquiry and, abashed, he nodded. "And that my real client is a very wealthy Frenchman by the name of Yvegeny de Saint Nerin."

"Oui. That is true." He looked completely unperturbed.

"And when were you going to inform me of that fact?" Helen demanded.

"Soon," he replied evenly.

She wasn't convinced. "I bet," she muttered. "So would you care to explain what happened back there?"

"Alexandrov," Guy said.

Yves nodded. "Oui, I think so, too."

Helen looked from one man to the other. "Who's Alexandrov?"

"A very ruthless businessman."

"Is there any other kind?" Her tone was crisp and tart.

Yves looked at her sharply. "Whatever you may think of my deception, Helen, at least I don't go around threatening my rivals with physical violence."

"Is that what he did to you?" Helen should have been aghast, but she had heard too many similar stories over the years to feel surprised.

"If he only restricted himself to threats against me, I could cope. But he threatened my family, also."

Helen saw a quick expression of cold fury shift across Yves' face and shivered. She wouldn't ever want to be on the other side of that reaction from him.

"Your family?"

Yves looked too angry to continue, so Guy stepped in with the explanation. "The villa of Monsieur's sister in Lyon caught on fire a few days before our departure for Australia."

"Was anyone hurt?" Helen asked, stunned. Business rivalry was one thing, but when someone deliberately targeted bystanders, that was unforgivable.

"Luckily, my sister and her children fled the house before they were harmed," Yves told her. "However, her husband holds me responsible for putting them in danger in the first place. And," he finished grimly, "I don't blame him."

"Is that why you're in Australia?" she asked slowly, putting two and two together in her head. "To avoid Alexandrov?"

Yves smiled briefly in appreciation. "You're a very astute woman, Helen. Yes, I was afraid Alexandrov might continue to harass those close to me if I remained. He appears to work best with an audience, so I determined to deny him one."

"And what about the deal with Tech-88?"

"That is legitimate business. I just moved the timetable forward several weeks."

Helen absently reached for one of the sandwiches on the plate in front of her, munching on it thoughtfully.

"I still don't think I understand," she remarked. "What will two weeks in Australia achieve if this Alexandrov person has already managed to track you here?"

She supposed a logical enough course of action would be to fly back to France which, after all, was home territory for Yves. She didn't want him to leave, realised with a sharp pang that, despite his deception, there was still something about this man that she found irresistible, but she wouldn't be doing her job as someone hired to protect him, if she failed to mention a viable option for them both. How could she live with herself if she didn't mention it, and something happened to him?

"He can't be sure," Yves explained. "I had to shake Alexandrov up by going some place he didn't expect me to be. My only disappointment is that he managed to track Guy and I so quickly. I was hoping we would have at least a week of peace before something happened."

So that's what he meant when he spoke of a little peace during their evening together.

All we have is a little time before chaos descends on us, Helen. Within a few days, news will no doubt spread that a European company is seeking a partnership with an Australian firm. And, when that happens, attention may well fall on our little party, and you may be forced to earn every euro of that paycheque we've given you, hm?

He hadn't really been referring to the partnership when he spoke of attention falling on them. He was referring to Alexandrov. And she had certainly earned her day's pay by quickly despatching their two attackers an hour ago.

"Why did you stop me contacting the police?" she asked. "I thought you'd want more protection, considering Alexandrov's tracked you down sooner than you anticipated."

"I know from my police contacts in Europe that they're building a case against Leonid Alexandrov. They are very close to gathering all the evidence they need." He lifted a jet black eyebrow. "It appears I am not the only person he has made it his business to harass. But I also know that Alexandrov has his own friends in high places. I came to Australia so my family would remain safe. But I cannot tell the police that I'm here and need protection because then I will be formally identified. The police will track my movements–"

"–and keep the police in Europe informed, and Alexandrov will be able to pin down where you are more accurately," she finished and blushed at the smile of delight he shot her.

"Exactement. Of course, it works both ways. Do we know for sure that those two young thugs came from him? Non. But, on the other hand, does he now know for sure that someone from my party despatched them? A woman, with two men? Non, again."

"So what do we do now?" she asked. "My personal recommendation would be to leave. Tonight."

"Leave Heritage House?" Guy asked.

Helen shook her head. "Leave Brisbane completely. Go someplace else where he won't be able to track you so easily."

"I will not do that," Yves interrupted. "I think the risk of staying here is acceptable."

Helen disagreed. "I don't. You've already said that this man tried to harm your sister and family and that he's wanted by police all over Europe. Why would you think it's an acceptable risk to remain where he can easily track you down?"

"I'm sure it will take a while for him to learn of what has happened to his messengers. And, as I said, we're not completely sure that those men came from him."

"They knew you when they saw you," Helen said darkly. "I saw the expressions on their faces. Alexandrov might have even sent them pictures of you, just so they'd be sure. In fact," she added, looking around quickly, "we don't know that they didn't follow us from Heritage House. Just because I didn't notice them before, doesn't mean they weren't around."

Her voice was bitter. Already she felt she had failed in her assignment. She'd had time to think about it while she'd showered the events of the morning from her skin. How would two people, obviously looking for Yves and Guy, know that they would be in New Farm? They wouldn't, unless they followed them from Heritage House in the first place. And whose fault was it that they weren't spotted at that point? Hers, of course. Hers, because that was what she was paid for and, instead of concentrating on her job, she was reliving wonder moments in bed with her client. Not even the client's secretary, but the client himself. At that moment, Helen wished the earth would open up and swallow her whole.

"Speaking of which, I'd like to commend you on your actions," Yves said to her, breaking into her morbid thoughts.

Helen looked up, alarmed. Was he making fun of her? But his face was serious, and his voice sounded sincere.

Guy shook his head in wonder. "You took care of them." He snapped his fingers. "In seconds. One moment, they were coming around the corner. And the next—poof!—they were two marionnettes on the ground with their strings cut."

"You handled them most competently, Helen," Yves added. "The reputation of Mr. Greenwood is not overstated."

Ryan! As if her situation weren't bad enough, what would Ryan say, knowing how badly she had messed up. Maybe it was just as well she was making so much money out of Yves, because she was sure Ryan would never trust her with such an important assignment again.

"I still think you should leave," she said stubbornly. "It's obvious to me that they already know you're here. And you really don't know how long it will take before Alexandrov tries again."

"The man already has enough on his plate," Yves replied. "I'm sure we'll be left alone, maybe even long enough to conclude our negotiations."

"You're being stupid."

The words hung in the air between them, and Helen felt a white-hot shaft of fury directed at her, searing her with its touch. Oh my. She had just managed to make an enemy of Yves de Saint Nerin, one of the richest men in Europe, according to what Sue told her.

Yves didn't even turn his head. "Guy, leave us."

The young assistant hurried from the room, throwing Helen a sympathetic look from behind Yves' back.

"So," Yves said silkily when the door clicked shut and they were alone, "would you care to repeat what you just said?"

"You're pinning all your hopes for safety on me," Helen argued in half-desperation. "Thanks for your confidence, but I can't replace round-the-clock police escorts, nor can I stay awake twenty-four hours a day. If you won't go to the police—"

"It is my opinion that would make things worse," he cut in.

"—or leave Brisbane—"

"Again, that is not possible. I have legitimate business here."

"—then why not hire another of Ryan's security escorts? Then there will be two of us looking after you instead of one. It would certainly make me feel better," she added.

He paused at that, leaning back while he considered her words.

"I don't want to bring another person into this," he said finally to her continuing exasperation. "Already, I feel too many people know Guy and my whereabouts."

He held up one lean, tanned finger when she was about to protest. "However, I will consider what you have said and give you an answer within the next day or so."

"And what if something happens between now and then?" Helen shot back. "I don't think you realise exactly how much danger you could be in."

Yves pushed back the chair and got to his feet. "Are you about to call me stupid again?" he asked angrily.

She mirrored the action, even though she still stood almost a head shorter than him. "I might," she retorted.

He paused and shook his head in wonder, a small smile on his face. "You have spirit," he said quietly. "Foolish, perhaps, but with spirit."

"I—"

She stopped. What could she say? His mind seemed to jump from one place to another, defying her attempts to predict what he was going to say next. All she could do was look at him helplessly.

"You're going to say we shouldn't have gone out for dinner last night."

"We shouldn't have gone out for dinner," she told him emphatically, and meant it...in all its possible interpretations.

"In that case, if future meals outside are out of the question," he asked, his voice dark and smooth, "should I not get some compensation for being stuck here?"

"I...I'm not sure what you mean," she stammered. Suddenly the room seemed charged with electricity, and Helen had difficulty drawing breath into her lungs.

"You are such a hard taskmistress," he said, stepping up to her. "And I am willing to obey you. Shouldn't I get a reward for that?"

Your reward is your life, she wanted to say. But, like her breath, her words stuck in her throat.

"Just a kiss," he whispered, his head lowering to hers. "As a sign of appreciation for my compliance."

It was madness. She had a job to do, and that job didn't entail indulging in passionate clinches with her paying client. She couldn't. She shouldn't, especially after what happened last time they kissed. She...

She was lost.

As his lips met hers, she couldn't help but give herself up to his embrace. She knew what a bad idea it was, but she needed Yves the way a plant needed sunshine, the way a butterfly needed wings. As his arms tightened around her, every logical reason why this was a bad idea fled completely. In this, she was weak, so weak, but she couldn't help herself, especially when she thought of how close he had been to harm.

She breathed in his scent as his tongue explored her mouth, running lightly along her teeth before thrusting himself deeper. She felt her body lift off the ground, until only her toes rested on the carpet, and she clung to him with frantic and questing fingers, grabbing his hair in a spasm of longing, as if she would never let go.

They were pressed so closely together that she could feel his burgeoning erection against her, and felt an answering wetness in her groin.

Everything about Yves was mesmerising — from his scent to the feel of his arms pressing against her back; from the sign of his physical desire for her to the silky black of his hair, and the way his jaw roughened against her smooth skin, textured and arousing. Helen wanted to feel that roughness roam all over her body, rubbing against her neck, breasts and thighs. She imagined him there, at her groin, the slick wetness of his tongue contrasting with the coarseness of a day-old beard, and just the thought of those textures touching her so intimately was enough to send a shudder through her body.

It didn't matter that she was throwing away her professional reputation. She wanted this man more than she had wanted anyone else in her life.

Even Peter?

The thought of the young instructor who had so tragically lost his life was enough to throw cold water on her heated fantasies. With an indrawn, panicked breath, Helen pulled away, quickly disengaging her hands from around Yves' neck and stepping back. She was expecting him to look cool and imperturbable, but his hair was ruffled, his eyes dark with desire, and she heard the unevenness of his breathing, a mirror to her own. She wondered if she looked anything near as discomposed as he did—she certainly felt it—and the thought shamed her.

She ran a shaking head through her blonde locks not meeting his eyes.

"I believe," she told him, "we've reached the end of our discussion."

She didn't see the expression on his face, but heard the promise in his reply.

"For now," he said. "For now."

* * * *

Yves wasn't quite sure he'd correctly heard the words from Helen's mouth. He looked from her to Guy. Night had fallen and they were seated on the wide verandah facing the river. The ripples from the water picked up the reflections from the office towers further upstream, making them glitter and dance in the warm air.

The staff from Heritage House had set up a small rectangular table, lighting its length with candles. This was the result of another compromise between him and Helen. She had wanted dinner to be inside, with all curtains drawn. He thought that was an overreaction and wanted to enjoy the weather of the city he was visiting. In the end, they had settled on an outside venue with flickering illumination. Helen joked that their greatest fear was a drive-by boat guided by gangsters with machine guns, but he saw the thought troubled her, and so acquiesced without further argument.

But now, halfway through their main meal — a superbly cooked steak with steamed and buttered vegetables — Helen had come out with a statement that had him staring at her in disbelief. He had, of course, known women who were determined to hook their claws into him on a more permanent basis, but even they had not been so blatant. Was she trading on her performance earlier on in the day in order to grab a more permanent meal ticket? The thought was as repugnant as it was sudden. And, unfortunately, it made all too much sense.

"Pardon?" he asked, slowly putting his fork and knife down on the fine porcelain plate. "Did you just say you want to sleep with me?"

Not that Yves was averse to the idea, not at all, but he expected — and usually received — more discretion than what was currently being exhibited. A curl of anger threaded through him at her impudence in mentioning intimacy at all around his assistant. Of course Guy knew how his life ran; after all, the young man was responsible for organising most of it himself. But this bald statement, at an otherwise light and pleasant meal, was beyond the realms of good taste, even if it involved a woman that he found more fascinating than any other he had met.

At least she had the grace to look a little abashed, he thought, watching her. But there was still no excuse for what she had just said.

"I didn't say I want to sleep with you," she corrected. "I said you should not sleep alone."

Yves glanced at Guy, but he looked as confused as Yves himself felt. "I'm afraid the subtle difference between those two statements escapes me," he said coolly. "Perhaps you'd care to explain it yourself."

Helen took a deep breath. "You sleep in the downstairs suite, don't you?"

"Oui." He shrugged. "I like strolling into the garden in the morning. It's a nice contrast to the hotels Guy and I normally frequent."

"Well, what if Alexandrov decides to send a couple more men after you?"

She stared at him with those big eyes of hers, shaded now by the low illumination but still large and engaging. He thought of naked swims in some exotic lagoon, feeling topaz blue waters engulf his body, and had to force himself away from those thoughts.

"You're saying they could break into my suite." Of course, it was obvious to him now.

Helen nodded. "You refuse to give me an answer on hiring more security, and I'm presuming you'll refuse to change suites." He nodded curtly at her assumption. "So, the only option left is to not let you sleep alone."

He should have known better than to think she had her own sexual agenda. The kiss they'd exchanged earlier that day convinced him that Helen Collier was a woman fighting herself as much as she was fighting him. He didn't know exactly what it was that stopped her from succumbing to his last kiss, but it was something sad and personal — not a promise but an experience. An abusive old boyfriend? Certainly she could take care of herself now — he still marvelled when he thought of the way she had so neatly despatched their two attackers — but had she been like that in the past? Maybe her independence grew out of a need for protection. The idea of someone hurting Helen made him draw in a quick breath, but he could be working on a false assumption. Maybe it was something more recent. In any case, he would make it his business to find out the reason...and soon. His body remembered the imprint of her curves against him, hot and smooth. He wanted a repeat of that night. Badly. And he was determined to cut through her resistance in order to sate his need.

"Are you inviting yourself to my bedroom?" Now that he was sure of her motives, he could relax and tease her a little. It surprised him how much pleasure he got from doing it, enjoying the look of embarrassment that slowly bloomed on her face. In truth, he found her usual self-discipline formidable, and liked to uncover the warm and attractive woman that he knew existed under all that serious focus. Helen was too lively a person to be buried under such crushing responsibility. As what he was now putting onto her, he realised with a pang.

"I'm sure we'll come to some arrangement that offers us both some privacy," she replied shortly.

Yves dabbed at his mouth with the corner of his linen napkin, hiding a smile. "I'm sure we will."

Why was he being so frivolous about his personal safety? Even Guy had alluded to it earlier in the day, while they were finalising their agenda for the business meeting the following day. He was usually a cautious man and events had already indicated that Leonid Alexandrov was not a person one lightly crossed. While it was true that he was half a world away from his home, Alexandrov had already found him soon enough. What Helen had suggested throughout the day was logical and sensible, yet he still refused to listen to her.

It wasn't that he didn't believe Helen because she was a woman. In fact, and he startled himself by admitting this, it was the complete opposite. There was something about being with her that was out of time, out of his normal experience. And he didn't want it to end. It was as simple as that. He didn't want another bodyguard, as sensible as that idea was, because he didn't want another person intruding on the dynamic currently at play. Guy had been his assistant for several years now and was able to competently read the non-verbal wishes of his employer. And Helen was the woman he wanted to currently pursue. Yes, it was foolish and selfish, and he knew he might pay a heavy price for it, but he didn't want anyone else around. For a start, he knew Helen was serious enough to use any newcomer as a shield against him. Further, if the extra bodyguard turned out to be Ryan Greenwood himself then Helen might as well be locked within a bank vault.

The ideal situation would be to hire someone extra, see through this trip in peace, then pay another visit to Australia in the future when the situation had been resolved to his satisfaction, and he could sleep peacefully again, knowing that Alexandrov was in jail where he belonged. But Yves knew the hectic pace of his own schedule. The hurried nature of this particular trip meant that several important meetings had been shoved to one side. The resultant jam of appointments resembled an accordion, pressed up close to one another for the next few months. It was an impossible situation.

Non, whatever he wanted to do with Helen, he had to do now with as few distractions as possible. Even if it meant that his personal danger increased. Yves' own sense of confidence was based on what he knew of Alexandrov's character. The reason the man had approached him in the first place was because of their common Russian heritage. Yves' grandmother had fled Russia at the cusp of the Revolution as a child with her aristocrat parents, and their standing in society had only been strengthened through subsequent marriages into French society. Alexandrov, a social climber himself, found the combination irresistible. When he met Yves, he insisted on a partnership based on what he termed 'blood ties', meaning Russian blood. Before he rejected the financial overtures, Yves had had the Russian investigated, and knew how the man thought.

Alexandrov was known not to trust people in general, so he would not leave the intimidation of a business rival, especially someone he perceived to be a fellow Russian, who had turned him down, to any run-of-the-mill criminal gang. The way he operated, Leonid would always go looking for the personal touch. And that meant tapping into the local Russian population. Yves hadn't told even Guy, but he had investigated the size of that potential local group before they left Grenoble, and was relieved to see it numbered only in its hundreds. There was a risk that he was wrong, of course, but Yves doubted that such a small population produced professional killers, eager to do the bidding of a dangerous criminal thousands of kilometres away. The two who had attacked them in New Farm were exactly what he expected—young and inexperienced, possibly even broke—and he wasn't anticipating any further opposition to be too different.

He had meant to make that observation to Helen, but the day had been too busy, and now she suggested that she sleep in his bedroom? Yves hadn't risen to his current level of success by ignoring the potential of situations. And he wasn't going to start now.

Chapter Seven

He was a stubborn man, and she wanted to kick him. Why someone supposedly as successful and smart as he was, couldn't see that it would be better for all concerned — herself included — if he hired another bodyguard was beyond her. It wasn't that he was a miser; the fact that he rented out Heritage House entirely, just for his and Guy's initial residence proved that. But she just couldn't get over this particular example of his pigheadedness.

Helen grabbed a pair of jogging pants and tank top from her dresser with a sharp yank. It couldn't be that he actually wanted to spend some time in her company. Not after her last rebuff. She was sure Yves de Saint Nerin was used to much easier conquests, and he had probably put her in the 'too hard' basket by now.

She walked to the bathroom to start getting ready for the night. The fact of the matter was, she wanted someone else around, as a distraction if nothing else. She was unnerved by the intensity of Yves' looks, as if she was a delectable morsel that he wanted to savour.

Her resolve failed her at times like that, because she wanted to be savoured by him and feel the hard muscles of his body next to hers. That first night of lust with him had kick-started all kinds of distracting and unproductive thoughts, and, rather than getting her fill of him, she wanted more. Maybe if someone else was around, it would give her time to put the relationship on a more rational footing, but he remained stubborn and obstinate in that regard. Damn the man!

How much easier it would be if she wasn't paid to guard him, but could just be his female companion for a while. His mistress? Helen had never ever seen herself in such a position but now, for the first time in her life, she understood what drove women to become the kept companions of men. If they looked and acted like Yves de Saint Nerin, with his abundance of charm, good looks and wealth, then it was no surprise that women were prepared to give up only their principles to be with them. Given half a chance, Helen didn't doubt that she might do that herself.

And that brought her back full circle. She briefly thought of just calling Ryan anyway and explaining why she needed him — now! — on the job with her, but she wasn't the client. She didn't have the authority to do such a thing. Just strongly suggest it but not do it.

Helen finished brushing her teeth. After rinsing and drying her mouth, she pulled on the pants and shimmied into the jewel-toned tank top, brushing back her hair before finally giving up in exasperation. Her blonde locks were just what they were, and there was no use trying to wish them into something else. She looked at herself in the mirror, noting her too-bright eyes and the flush that delicately outlined her cheekbones. Her body was looking forward to this with a longing that went beyond decency. She shook her head and the reflection in the mirror had the grace to look rueful. Her suggestion to spend the night in Yves' suite was the right one to make, and she would have made it regardless of whether she was paid to guard an old, fat, businessman or Yves himself. She just wished she could be a bit more objective about the looming situation.

With set lips and a determined tilt to her chin, Helen walked the length of Heritage House, leaving the refuge of her own suite and, after a perfunctory knock, entering Yves' territory.

She heard the shower running as she neared the main bedroom, and briefly wondered what to do before her feet took over, walking her through the door, past the bathroom and over to the sofa that sat between the bed and the doors leading out to the balcony. Logically, this would be where she spent her night. Boldly going through the closet, she managed to find a spare pillow and a blanket and was making up her bed on the sofa when the bathroom door opened.

Wincing, she shut her eyes for a moment then forced an impersonal expression on her face and turned to face Yves.

This is nothing you haven't seen before, Hel. Plus you used to train with a whole squad of buff males, remember? They used to walk half-naked around you all the time, dripping testosterone like some expensive aftershave. You never even noticed them after a while.

But those were just her training partners. None of them, not even Pete — at the start of their friendship — had elicited the kind of response Helen felt zapping through her body right now.

His hair was still damp and long enough to form attractive spikes that dripped errant drops of water down the side of his face. Helen swallowed and followed the progress of one such drop, watching as it clung to his skin, rolled down the taut brown of his throat, over his collarbone and into the thin mat of dark hair that covered his chest. The drop was lost, but her gaze continued downwards, over a well-toned torso and a fine narrow dusting of fuzz that arrowed downwards beneath the blazing white towel that encircled his hips. His entire body was an even nut-brown, a detail she hadn't noticed before, much to her shame, indicating that he sunbathed–

"So you are determined to do this?" he asked.

The light behind him was still on, so it was difficult seeing his full expression, but Helen heard the amusement in his voice. The small smile that quirked one side of his gorgeous lips was only just visible.

She turned back to the sofa and plumped the pillow. "It's part of my job," she said pertly.

Silence pooled in the room, and Helen knew he was watching her. She felt his gaze bore into her back.

"It won't be very comfortable on that sofa," he finally remarked, his voice casual.

"I think it'll do just fine," she replied, still not facing him. She picked up the blanket, that was only slightly in disarray, shook it open and started folding it again.

"If I promise to be a gentleman," that voice of chocolate went on, "would you consider sleeping in the bed with me? Only sleeping," he reassured quickly. "The bed is big, and I could put a pillow between us if it would make you feel better."

He was being so nice, so gallant, that Helen felt like a shrew with her back still facing him. She threw down the blanket with a sigh and turned around. The truth of the matter was, it wasn't him she was worried about, it was herself. She wouldn't put it past her suddenly over-wound libido to jump a fence of razor-wire that separated her from Yves, especially if it was situated on a piece of furniture as tantalising and full of possibility as a bed. All it would take would be one careless flick of a limb, or the smell of his warm body slumbering close to hers. It was going to be difficult enough settling nearby. But both of them in the same bed together? Impossible.

"Thank you," she finally said, trying to muster some semblance of graciousness in her reply, "but I think it would be for the best if I sleep here tonight."

He walked over to his dresser and pulled out a drawer.

Oh God, he's going to change in front of me!

Her cheeks flaming, Helen spun away from him. Suddenly, the neutral tones of the linen curtain absorbed all her attention. But with Yves' shadow projected onto the fabric, together with the accompanying sounds, Helen might as well have been watching him directly.

She heard the slither of material as something was pulled from the drawer, and a clunk as it was pushed back in. Yves shook it out and Helen saw the bulk of a pair of pants...they must be pyjama pants. Probably with stripes—cool, blue stripes that lengthened his legs and looked serious and sexy all at the same time. She wanted them to have a different pattern — stupid hearts or hairy black monkeys cavorting all over it — but knew her luck wouldn't hold. There was nothing in the room to laugh at.

A quick flick sent the towel flying onto the bed. Helen saw the unmistakable shape of a discarded towel with her peripheral vision, and her eyes widened.

He's completely naked now, all that length of man on full display. I wonder if I could sneak a look. Oh God, if only I could sneak a look!

Then the slither of his legs as he put on the pants. He reached for the towel that lay on the bed.

"You can turn around now," he said, and it was plain he was laughing at her. Most probably the women of his acquaintance kept watching when he changed, yearned to be there while he discarded all clothing. Did they drool, she wondered, or just smack their lips in anticipation? Here he was, thousands of kilometres from home, and instead of some open admiration, his tough, no-nonsense bodyguard behaved as though she was a priggish, born-again virgin.

"I believe in giving all my clients a sense of privacy and respect," she said, trying to explain her actions.

"I'm in no doubt of that, Helen." He rubbed his hair with the end of the towel. "I'm going to put this towel back then brush my teeth. I'll be five minutes."

Helen nodded stiffly, not trusting herself to speak, waiting until he disappeared into the bathroom once again, shutting the door behind him, before she relaxed.

"Stupid, stupid, stupid," she railed at herself in an angry whisper. "He's only a man, for God's sake. Okay, so you want to jump his bones. But you can't. You had your chance, and that's all you get. He's a paying client, and you have a job to do." She moved the pillow to the opposite end of the sofa, so she wouldn't see him walk back into the bedroom when he was done.

"Besides, he's out of your league," she muttered as she slapped the blanket, still annoyed. "He hires and fires people like you."

She pulled her mobile from the pocket of her track pants, checked the charge then laid it with a click on the glass-topped side table next to the sofa.

By the time Yves walked back into the bedroom, she was settled under the blanket, looking and feeling a little more composed. The thick blackout curtain linings cancelled all light from the balcony outside. When he switched off the bathroom light, the room was plunged into pitch blackness.

"There's still room in the bed, if you want."

Somehow, it was easier to stick to her guns when she couldn't see him. The task was merely difficult instead of being almost impossible.

"Goodnight, Mr. de Saint Nerin."

"Yves," he corrected, and it was a sensual whisper in the darkness.

"Goodnight...Yves," she finally said and prepared for a night of sleeplessness.

* * * *

She was warm and soft, and her prickles were nowhere in sight. Yves smiled in the darkness as he carried Helen's sleeping form to the bed. He had heard her toss and turn on the thin, awkwardly shaped sofa, and his sense of chivalry would not let him fall back into slumber while his small protector was in such discomfort.

Non. Who was he kidding? The fact was, he wanted Helen Collier with a need that was all-consuming, and he had barely a handful of days left before he had to leave the country. Who knew when he would find the time to come back? And, in the meantime, there was a strong, giving woman who was fighting herself as well as him. Yves only hoped she was exhausted enough from the struggle to yield to his enticements.

He laid her carefully in the middle of the bed. His eyes had grown used to the lack of light in the room, but she was still little more than a shadowed outline. Slowly, he lowered himself down next to her, his head just by her feet. With a wicked grin, he kissed her instep. There was no response and Yves quirked an eyebrow. He kissed her instep again, and flicked a tongue against her ankle.

Helen moaned and moved her foot away, shifting sideways on the bed, one leg kicked up as she made herself comfortable. In a nimble move, Yves settled behind her, spooning her as he shuffled close to her body. He knew he shouldn't be doing this. And normally, he never had to resort to such actions in order to literally get a woman into his bed. But, in addition to being a spicy challenge, Helen appealed to something deep inside of him. Her spirit and intelligence increased the lust he felt for her. No, it was more than lust—Yves knew that much—but he wasn't going to think about it. There was still Alexandrov in the back of his mind. The broken relationship with his sister and brother-in-law that he had to mend. The rest of his business empire to look after.

At that moment, he wished he was someone else. An uncomplicated associate of Ryan Greenwood's, for example. Or a fellow martial arts instructor. Anything that meant he could grab what was blossoming between him and Helen and spend enough time on it, with her, so some kind of resolution could be reached. Either an eventual drifting apart or...something else.

But he wasn't such a man. He had a business. Responsibilities. He would have to leave Helen when he went back to France. Which meant there was only the now. For both of them.

He stretched his hand around her ribs and cupped her breast, slowly pinching at the nipple through the thin material. Responding to his touch, it puckered in his hand, and that was enough to harden his cock. He increased the pressure slightly as he pushed against her back, his erection fitting neatly in the crease between her buttocks. Helen squirmed, making Yves groan. He knew the moment she woke when her body tensed against his.

"What—?"

"Non," he said quietly by her ear. "No questions. No thought. Just two adults. And a long, dark night."

"We can't." She shifted around, sending more torment through Yves' groin before she faced him. There was a respectable distance between them, with only his hand resting on her shoulder. There was also torment in her voice. "I can't, Yves. It was bad enough before, when I thought it was Guy, who was my employer."

"Regardless of who we are, we're attracted to each other," he countered softly.

"That may be true," she conceded, "but there are lives at stake here. Yours and Guy's."

His hand moved up her shoulder, caught a tendril of her hair and smoothed it against her head. "I wish I could explain this," he told her, the darkness making him honest. "There is some magic around you, enticing me, tempting me. Tell me you don't feel this as well, tell me this heat through my blood is only on my side, and I promise I'll let you sleep in peace."

"I...," she paused before she could utter her lie. "No," she finally admitted. "It's not just you. I feel it too."

And she hated herself for it. Helen didn't say the words, but Yves knew she was thinking them, and he wondered how a passionate woman had managed to so effectively close off part of herself like that. No more! No more thinking. No more running away.

He pulled her forward, tasting her lips gently, seducing her with tenderness. When she groaned, a small sound of capitulation, Yves pushed his advantage, tunnelling one hand along the mattress beneath her while his other moved under her tank top. Her nipple peaked against his fingers. She would have pulled back, but his arm was already there, holding her tight. Lifting himself on the elbow closest to the bed, he kissed her neck and felt her shiver against his mouth. Her tendons were taut, dipping into a shallow valley along her throat. With infinite care, Yves followed the inviting crease, smiling into her flesh as he felt her hands grab at him.

Swiftly, he lifted the edge of her tank top and suckled deeply on her. With a gasp, she arched against him, her fingers digging into him, urging him to pull her aroused nub deeper into his mouth and run his tongue over its heightened sensitivity. Yves was more than happy to oblige. He held her trembling body against his as he rolled her onto her back. Mindlessly, they both shucked their pants, and Yves' thick shaft bobbed against Helen's abdomen, softness against softness, slick with the thick drops of his lubrication. He nibbled, moving from one breast to the other, plumping their roundness in his hands, massaging one while he suckled on the other.

With heated impatience, he felt Helen pull the top up over her head, throwing it into the darkness, groaning as her naked body rubbed against his. She groaned with incoherent need, moving her legs apart in blatant invitation. , Yves moved away, but it was only to grab a condom from the bedside table drawer. He liberated the contents of the small packet with economical movements, and fitted it onto himself, letting his heavy, sheathed erection fall between her thighs, his engorged head brushing past her pubic thatch, the texture making him catch his breath. Every second of his time with Helen was crystal-clear in his mind, every brush of her against him etched on his body. Even without burying himself in her, it was a surfeit of sensation, threatening to topple him over the edge. Her strong fingers gripped him, meeting his rising passion with her own, demanding that he touch her, kiss her, lick her. He positioned his hips, pushed forward and gasped as his cock drowned in Helen's own slippery wetness. It was an invitation his body couldn't resist. Sliding into her was like being in the one place he belonged. Her curves and heat cradled him. Her tremors aroused him. He started moving, taking his weight on his elbows and brushing her hair back from her face. Under his fingertips, he felt her head move from side to side, and heard the gasps of pleasure emerging from her lips.

The darkness was almost complete, but his sense of sight was unnecessary. Every quiver of Helen's body told its own story, its building tension telling him of her imminent orgasm. Lifting himself onto his hands, he lowered his head and kissed her. She gasped into his mouth as his tongue flicked against hers. He increased the tempo of his body, driving into her as she wrapped her long, lithe legs around his body, meeting each thrust with one of her own. The shudders hit his body in a wave of surprise, an aching peak of pleasure that arched his back and stretched his throat, shouting his climax to the room. Beneath him, Helen was also in the throes of a tempest, shuddering against his groin, milking him of his semen as she bucked and cried out in the darkness of his bedroom.

* * * *

Helen's phone rang early the next morning, waking her from sleep. It was six in the morning, and she was momentarily disoriented. Her fingers ran over the padded outline of a mattress rather than a large sofa cushion. And there was a solid length of bulky arm holding her close. She moved her feet and held her breath when it encountered a leg.

Oh no! What have I done? Again!

Caught between a flood of sudden recollection, and the insistent ring of the phone, she stumbled out of bed. She was completely naked. Looking around frantically, she spied a robe casually thrown over a chair and carelessly threw it on, grabbing the phone and pressing a button with shaking fingers.

"Hello," she half-whispered, willing her voice to sound calm as she exited the bedroom. As she passed the bed, she saw the dark outline of Yves' body move under the covers, tried to imagine that it was something else, and quickened her step.

Ryan's bluff voice boomed in her ear. The man had always been an early riser, and it sounded as though he had already been up for hours.

"Hel, it's me," he said, without preamble. "Thought I'd check in with you. How's it going?"

Helen ran a distracted hand through her hair, trying to get her thoughts into order. Feeling damned guilty. She wondered if Ryan could feel the heat from her flushed cheeks buzzing through the air between their phones.

"Well," she cleared her throat, "first, the client was not exactly who we thought it was."

Knowing him as she did, she heard the question in his silence and, glad to be on impersonal ground, briefed him on the fact that it was Yves who was the real client not Guy Aubrac. Ryan grunted and explained that that was not an unknown tactic. Helen just raised her eyebrows as a personal editorial and continued, but Ryan's answers became less relaxed as she related the attack on them at New Farm.

"I don't know where to begin," he told her angrily after she finished. "Whether to front up and call Nerin a fool, or whether to wipe the floor with you for not calling the police."

"I think he had a good reason to do what he did," she replied, stung. "If he's right about this Alexandrov character having friends in law enforcement, then calling in the authorities could have made things worse."

She heard her mentor's long, bitter sigh down the receiver. "I still think it was bloody hare-brained of the both of you," he muttered, "but there's no help for it now. How stubborn is the man?"

Stubborn? The word had been invented with Yves specifically in mind.

"You have no idea," she breathed with a touch of amused asperity.

"Hmph. And what's your plan now?"

"We're due to have the first in a series of corporate meetings today."

"Is that with the computer company?"

"That's right." Helen shifted, uncomfortable with what she left unsaid.

"And Alexandrov's men have already seen you in New Farm and, from what you say, managed to track you from Heritage House."

"That's right." She winced, but kept her voice even.

"Great. And what if Alexandrov tries again?"

"Yves doesn't seem to rate that possibility very highly," she said slowly.

"Yves, is it?" Ryan paused, but Helen didn't answer. Had he heard the thread of feeling in her voice? She remained quiet and Ryan eventually conceded, filling in the silence. "Yves is the client. He's not supposed to think anything. That's your job."

"I know, but he's very —"

"Do you have a safe house?"

Helen thought up, and discarded, several choices. Another hotel? No, that would be easily traced. Her place in the Valley? No, that was obvious as well. A friend's? She couldn't do that, place friends in danger.

"Yes," she replied quickly, thinking of one other place she could go. "I have a place."

"Well, if something happens again, you get him there, then call me. No mobiles, not until we know what we're dealing with."

She took a deep breath. "Done. I'm sorry, Ryan. I know you put your trust in me —"

"A Russian criminal hell-bent on revenge is even a new one for me, Hel." His voice was gruff. "Just don't keep me in the dark from now on, okay?"

"Okay." She terminated the call and rested her head against the wall. If she could ignore her enormous pile of guilt at the moment, the conversation had not been as painful as she'd expected, and she was thankful that she and Ryan finally had a chance to talk. Events seemed to have flashed past in a whirl ever since she first stepped into Heritage House.

A voice at her ear made her jump.

"Was that Ryan Greenwood?" Yves asked, his head poking around the corner.

Helen used indignation to cover her embarrassment. "Were you eavesdropping on me?"

Yves shrugged. "You were outside the bedroom. And the door was open."

He looked alert but still a bit tousled, with his dark hair arranged chaotically and his pyjama pants—he had obviously put them on when he got out of bed, and Helen's mind ran riot at the thought—riding low on his hips.

She took a deep breath and brushed past him to walk into the bedroom again, picking up her watch and slowly latching it to her wrist. She could almost feel him follow her.

"Ryan just reminded me how foolish it was not to contact the police after that altercation yesterday," she said, closing her eyes. She didn't want to think about what had happened the night before—with her full consent. Once again, she had compromised her principles for a hunk of gorgeous man. Was she stupid? Or just besotted?

"But we agreed—"

"Yes, yes, I know," she interrupted, her voice rising. She spun to face him. "But he also reminded me that that's what you're paying me for. I'm the one who should decide where you go."

"A woman in charge?" his eyes gleamed. "I think I'd like that."

She ignored the implications in his statement. "One more attack, and we leave."

Yves sobered at that. "Where to?"

"A safe house."

He looked down at her, gauging the truth of her words. "You're serious, aren't you?"

"Yes, I am. Just as you should be," she rebuked.

He nodded and had the grace to look abashed. "Oui. I know. But I would not have been so adamant if I'd thought for a moment you or Guy had been in any great danger."

She wasn't quite sure how she felt about that. Was he saying that he had the utmost confidence in her ability to defend him? Or that he thought she was somehow being hysterical? Either way, it didn't matter. She was here to do a job and was happy that Ryan had given her a much-needed kick up the pants, even if she felt out of her depth. Her pleasure at the amount of money she was due to receive was tempered by the fact that, by the end of the two-week assignment, she was sure she would have earned every penny of it.

"If I was Leonid Alexandrov, I don't think I'd give up," she remarked, watching him. Trying to reduce him to a cipher. A client. Nothing more. Certainly not the man who had caused that delicious ache in her loins or that feeling of gentle lassitude.

"Alexandrov's reach doesn't stretch as far across the world as he'd like to think." Yves hesitated, as if debating whether to share something with her. "The Russian population in this city is small," he finally said. "I did my homework before we flew to Australia. I don't think Leonid will have much success finding killers to do his dirty work here."

"Russians aren't the only violent ones in this country," she countered.

"No, but that's the way Leonid likes to do business. He likes to keep things 'in the family', as he puts it. He believes it makes his messages more...personal."

She caught his gaze on her, intense and watchful, waiting for her reaction. He might be a wonderful businessman, she thought, but he was wrong to think that he could apply the logic of high finance and corporate life to emotion-laden issues. Maybe she wasn't as useless as she thought.

"I don't care," she said. "You could be right. But, then again, you could be wrong. And I don't like playing the odds when there are lives on the line."

Yves arched an eyebrow. "Do you know, Helen, I'm not sure I'm used to having anyone disagree with me on such a regular basis."

"Does it bother you?"

Her voice held an element of challenge, and he smiled. "Au contraire. I find it most refreshing."

It was his smile that did it—that lazy curve of lips that sent lightning zapping through the room, stinging Helen, and sending a small shiver up her spine. His smile told her exactly what he wanted to do with her, exactly how he wanted to explore her refreshing disagreement. She didn't dare even cast a glance at the bed, or she knew she'd be lost. Again.

"What time is the meeting with Tech-88?" she asked in a voice that was much calmer than the tumult in her stomach suggested.

"Nine-thirty." He paused. "We have plenty of time to get ready. Hours…to relax, have something to eat."

Go to bed.

The invitation hung, unsaid, between them.

He was here, offering himself to her—every inch of a sunbathed body, toned, muscular, hard. Eyes that saw into her soul, hands that held her tight, and lips that drove her to distraction. Who would have thought that Yves, just standing there, was enough to knock almost every ounce of sense from her body?

A compulsion gripped her, even sent her a half-step forwards, before sense reasserted itself. How she wanted to lose herself with that body, just one more time. To give his mouth free rein over her, to clutch and caress his hot, hard flesh. And maybe, if Ryan hadn't called that morning, they might have been staging a repeat performance even as she stood there. But her old teacher's words were still fresh in her mind, delivering a timely reminder of her responsibilities, and why exactly she—Helen Collier— was in a beautifully appointed suite with Yves de Saint Nerin.

There was nothing for her here. Not in the long term, in any case. He had not chosen her to be his companion, met her at a cocktail party, or traded words at a meeting together. They had been flung together through circumstance, with no rich families, or influential acquaintances in common. Much more than the mere geographic distance of half a world separated them. In fact, if it wasn't for Pete's tragic accident, she might not even be here at all, so fickle a player was fate.

"I have to get ready," she said, looking at the wall just to one side of him. "I...I'll see you for breakfast."

To his credit, he didn't try to stop her as she picked up her clothes and walked past him. But a part of her wished desperately that he would.

Chapter Eight

Helen didn't have much time to think on anything else for the rest of the day. She was on high alert from the moment they stepped out of the comfort of Heritage House. This time she didn't make the same mistake, she confidently installed herself in the front seat next to the driver of their limousine taxi, leaving Yves and Guy safely cushioned in the back. Her eyes scanned the surrounding roads as they drove, and she was glad she knew Brisbane so well. There wasn't a single deviation that the driver, a pleasant older man called Mick, could take without tipping her off that something was amiss. But the car made it to New Farm smoothly, and slipped noiselessly into the underground car-park of Tech-88. Unless they were perched behind the gauzy white curtains of surrounding houses, Helen didn't think anybody had watched for them.

She was dressed in dark pants and a lightweight matching jacket with a rust-coloured shirt underneath. Nothing about her outfit was too flashy or bright. Helen always thought of it as her 'waiter outfit', but it was comfortable, unobtrusive and allowed free movement. She didn't have the dark glasses or the Secret Service earphone, but her gaze was cool and competent as she swept the car-park, before beckoning the two men out of the back seat with a quick, economical wave of her hand.

Yves was no longer the man she wanted to rip the clothes off and ravage—Helen had locked up that part of herself tight while she had gotten ready that morning—but a very vulnerable, walking, talking target with bull's-eyes painted strategically on various parts of his body. And it was her job to make sure that he got on that plane back to France in the same condition as he had gotten here. For the first time, handling an easy security job that had suddenly turned deadly serious, she appreciated what Ryan went through every time one of his clients personally requested his services. She didn't envy him his job.

They were met upstairs by the smiling receptionist and shown into a large conference room that overlooked the bucolic backyard of the abutting house. Clothes fluttered on the drying lines, and clumps of flowers towered in cheerful bunches of yellow, pink and red. Helen looked beyond all of that, trying to spot someone who shouldn't be where they were, but the house and yard looked empty. She knew the office windows she gazed out of were tinted, but drew the vertical blinds across the expanse, angling them so they obscured vision but still let in some light, and ignored Yves' look of impressed amusement.

"I can wait outside, if you'd prefer," she remarked to both men.

"Non." That was Yves. "Stay here. I feel safer when you're around."

Although her face didn't show it, something deep inside warmed to those words, and she took a chair in the corner of the room, behind the row of chairs that surrounded the conference table.

Two other men entered the room, one of them with a slim laptop and the other with folders of papers. Helen remained unobtrusive, happy to be introduced then forgotten as the meeting began.

The man with the papers was in his mid-fifties. He was of medium height and a portly build, but sprightly with a direct voice that reminded her a lot of Ryan. He was the owner and founder of the company, and his name was Scott Nelson. The thick sheaves of paper he held, he explained, were the company's last three annual reports, as well as various white papers, case studies and several marketing plans that the company had commissioned. His blue eyes took in her presence with a flicker of surprise, but he quickly moved on and started talking business with Yves and Guy.

The second man was tall and thin, with short brown hair, and long skinny fingers. From his pallor, rare in the Brisbane sub-tropical climate, Helen knew he didn't get out very much. She would have been surprised if he even noticed there were other people in the same room as him. He was Ian McFarlane, Scott explained, and was one of the company's senior technical architects.

Ian set up the laptop in the centre of the table, set a presentation slideshow to run, and took a seat next to Scott.

If Helen had experience in running a small business, the following two hours showed her what it was like to run something substantially bigger. Both sets of men bandied around multi-million dollar figures with a casualness that was mind-boggling. They spoke of business opportunities in Italy, China, Canada and Thailand as if deals could be signed just by scurrying down the road, instead of after exhausting, transoceanic flights.

Yves showed a part of himself that Helen always knew lurked under the surface, but hadn't yet seen out in the open. He was polite but direct and ruthless in his curiosity. Naturally, with the deal between them not being completely sewn up, both Scott and Ian tried to keep some details of their company confidential, but Helen saw the way Yves would break the deflected query into several, smaller ones, arriving at the answer he wanted, but via a slightly more circuitous route. Did the Australian businessmen even realise they were being subtly and successfully interrogated, she wondered. She herself was more than a little intimidated by the easy confidence of his questioning.

By the end of the meeting, she was as wrung out as any of the other four. But while they could now relax, she still had her job to do. Over handshakes, they agreed to go ahead with the partnership. Yves promised to obtain some information for them from his head office in Paris, and they set a date for the following week to sign the initial paperwork.

"I think this calls for a celebration," Scott said, clapping everyone except Helen on the back. He smiled warmly at her, though, and she smiled back. "How about dinner, my treat?"

"Surely that duty falls to me?" Yves interceded smoothly.

"You're in my country, Yves, accepting my hospitality." Scott was blunt and firm. "I won't take no for an answer. Ian will join us as well, won't you?"

Ian McFarlane looked up, blinking, from his screen and gave a rather absent-minded assent.

"Then it's settled. I know a terrific seafood place in the city." He named a small, but exclusive restaurant perched above the crowds along the pedestrian mall of Queen Street. "I'll make reservations for seven, if that suits you folk."

Yves smiled and nodded his head. "Merci. We would enjoy that very much."

"A reservation for five," Scott confirmed. "I'll see you tonight."

* * * *

This was usually the part of a deal that Yves enjoyed as much as the negotiations themselves. He'd had Guy transfer all information on Tech-88 to their laptops before they left France, and had pored over the information on the long flight to Australia. This gave Yves more than double the time he usually had when preparing for meeting with a new company, and he'd been confident when he'd walked into the conference room that morning.

But all he had seen were dry figures and words glowing on the screen, and he needed to talk to the company's owner to really be sure that this was something he wanted to invest in. Thankfully, neither Scott Nelson nor Ian McFarlane had disappointed. Yves had noticed the balance and brevity of the two-person team, and knew that Scott had done his homework on Yves as well. He knew enough, for example, to know that Yves detested talking through a phalanx of lawyers in order to get answers to questions. And he knew enough to have a technical representative from his company there, the highly intelligent but nerdish Ian, to explain—in perhaps slightly more tortuously technical detail than necessary—the framework of the contracted works they were designing and implementing in countries throughout the region.

With the initial meeting of just two on two, both parties were able to speak relatively freely, and Yves liked what he heard and saw. Tech-88 would be a valuable addition to the Nerin group, and serve as a solid stepping-stone to future business in this lucrative part of the world.

Whichever way he looked at it, the meeting had been a success. Now, all that was required was to pass along some financial data and assurances from his side, prior to the signing of an initial understanding the following week. After that, the lawyers on both sides would take over, and the deal would be done— perhaps not as swiftly as Yves would have liked, but done nonetheless. He had achieved everything he wanted to, and Scott was inviting them to dinner to celebrate, as per the usual process in negotiations such as these. So why wasn't he happy about it? He normally enjoyed the socialising that accompanied the business—it was a way of cementing a young relationship. But he felt bored and a little irritated and even considered somehow bowing out of the dinner and letting Guy handle it on his behalf. Not that that was a contemplation for more than a second. For one, it would be unforgivably rude, and Yves prided himself on being a courteous professional. Secondly, the socialising was as important as the business.

He watched absently as Helen led the way from the conference room and down to where their limo was waiting, trying to figure out why he was so reluctant to attend dinner. His gaze sharpened as he realised exactly what the reason was. It was her. He gazed upon her straight back and the determination on her face as she looked from side to side, watching each person who even approached the invisible boundary that he knew she had drawn around them. She was so unlike the usual women of his acquaintance that he could hardly fathom it. For one, she had a level of self-control that he had never experienced before. Yves didn't consider himself arrogant...well, maybe slightly arrogant, he thought with a quick twitch of his lips. He knew women considered him attractive, with his combination of looks, wit and wealth. It was the task of seconds to attract a beautiful woman and charm her over dinner before slaking their mutual thirst in bed that night. He had done so, time and time again, whether he was at the gaming tables in Monaco or skiing the Alps in Switzerland. Yet, with this lithe, blonde Australian, it seemed not to be working at all. Oh, not the bed part. Although more difficult than his usual companions, she could no more resist the sizzling chemistry between them than he could. No, it was more than that. It was, despite the fact that they had tumbled in bed together—twice—that he wanted her more. Again. Still. Next to his usual conquests, this was tantamount to heresy.

Why? How? What was inside her that did not seem to be inside every other woman he had bedded then put to one side? Why, at this moment, was he thinking of her instead of his business?

He was quiet on the drive back to Heritage House, knowing that Guy would conclude that he was just tidying up details of the Tech-88 deal in his mind. But nothing was farther from his thoughts. In fact, his thoughts had moved on to another woman. Delphine de Rosanbo. His friend.

In a way, Helen reminded him of Delphine. They were both of a similar build and height, but that was the end of their physical likeness. Delphine had straight, silky dark hair and a complexion that didn't dare allow the presence of even a single sun-kissed freckle. She was charming in her own way, slightly aloof, independently wealthy and of unimpeachable character. She was also the woman Yves had, until that very moment, considered marrying.

The de Rosanbo and de Saint Nerin families had a long history of friendship together, although Delphine's bloodline was a lot bluer and more Gallic than Yves'. Still, Delphine had never evinced any kind of discrimination on that part. She was intelligent, socially adroit and beautiful. They had dinners together as often as they could, when their busy schedules placed both of them in the same city at the same time, and had laughed over the trials of finding partners, who loved them for themselves rather than the size of their bank accounts. It was that frivolous subject that had started them both thinking. There was no great passion between them, but both had agreed that passion was vastly overrated. They liked, and respected, each other, and Yves couldn't think of any other woman he'd consider as the mother of his children. Because there would be children, of course. He was quite sure on that count. If a woman's biological clock was loud and unrelenting, he felt that a man's was more subtle, perhaps more easily overlooked, but still there.

The discussion of a marriage between them was conducted in much the same way as their friendship — in slices of time when they could both meet, with humour, logic and grace. The time frame was set sooner rather than later, perhaps even within the next twelve months.

And it all went flying out of Yves' head the moment Helen had confronted their two young, male attackers and sent them tumbling into the bitumen. He hadn't said much at the time — had been too worried about any injuries to Helen and too surprised by the swiftness with which Alexandrov had found him — but he kept replaying the scene over and over in his mind.

It was like watching a deadly ballet. He had been there, himself, at the receiving end of one of her painful and intimate touches, her face, her lips, so close to his, as they followed his falling body to the ground. But that had been a caress compared to what she'd done to those two men. She'd moved in so close, that he'd thought she was attempting an embrace, the prelude to a kiss, then those hands of hers had moved in a blur. His ears had registered the soft sound of flesh colliding with hard surfaces, then they were both down, sprawled unconscious in the dirt. He'd never thought he would ever think it, but it had been wondrous, très magnifique! And suddenly, every woman he had known paled into insignificance, even beautiful, accomplished and supremely self-contained Delphine.

There was nothing self-contained about Helen. She tried to appear that way with those wary blue eyes the colour of crashing surf and her straight, sometimes abrupt, posture. But, like those errant blonde curls that constantly escaped their confines, she could not hide the passion that beat beneath a carefully cultivated exterior. Yves only had to watch her fight to see it emerge from her, like a terrible avenging angel. A passion she had matched in bed.

They got back to Heritage House, and Yves excused himself with a couple of quick remarks, heading back to his own suite and booting the laptop that sat on the desk. There was the information he had promised Scott, but he also had a strong urge to email Delphine. She would think it strange, uncharacteristic, to hear from him, but he couldn't help himself. He needed to hear from her, for what reason exactly, he couldn't fathom. Without thinking any more on it, he penned her a quick, impersonal email, ostensibly asking if she knew how Adrienne and the family were, and whether Theron was taking good care of them. The question was spurious — Yves knew his brother-in-law might not like him very much, but Adrienne and their children were like the sun and moon to him, and he would defend them to his dying breath. Still, he felt strange contacting Delphine without some kind of excuse, but what was the alternative? To put his thoughts down as baldly, and as badly, as they echoed in his head?

Dear Delphine,

I find myself in a quandry, my dearest friend. I am confused about so many things. But, first, I have a most urgent question. Can you tell me? What is love?

She'd have him committed to an asylum the moment he touched foot on French soil again if he wrote down such words. And not without justification.

Grimacing, he sent off the unsatisfactory email with a click of his mouse and put his troubled thoughts to one side, requesting that his Paris staff get together what was necessary and have it couriered to Scott in Australia straight away. He skimmed the rest of the emails that awaited his attention, noting that Guy took care of most of the more mundane matters, leaving the important decisions to him. His broker had written, informing him of the latest state of one of his portfolios and making a particular recommendation. The head of his electronics division informed him of the costs and benefits of relocating a factory to a different site. There was more, lots more, on matters he would have been happy to wrestle with in previous times. But not now. He didn't want to have dinner with Scott Nelson or Ian McFarlane, and neither did he want to spend time on the phone talking about any particular stock or acquisition recommendation.

He thrust back his chair and paced the suite's living room. He needed to get out, to work off some of his excess energy. But, of course, Helen would veto that idea in a moment. She was being paid to look after his physical well-being not help dissipate his restless roil of emotions, and that meant keeping him in a secured environment as much as possible. Even now, she was probably camped outside his suite, or positioned close to the sliding doors, behind the curtains that he kept drawn in deference to her wishes.

He walked over to the curtains and drew them back savagely. He understood Helen's concerns, but he wasn't a child. And maybe he didn't have her level of expertise, but he was sure that, in a normal kind of brawl, he could easily take care of himself.

Outside, the day was mellowing into afternoon. Scott Nelson had laid on an impressive mini-banquet during their morning meeting, and Yves knew his stomach could wait until dinner. Idly, he wondered what Helen was up to, because she wasn't visible on the terrace outside his suite. He flicked the catch on the door and stepped outside...and immediately felt the weight of someone's gaze upon him.

Slowly, Yves turned to his right. Helen, seated in a chair halfway along the verandah, nodded urbanely to him. He let out a breath of exasperation and walked over to her.

"Have you been here long?" he asked, noticing with irritation that she was still in what he would always think of as her uniform — dark pants, thin jacket, and a blouse underneath.

"No," she replied evenly. "Just since we returned from Tech-88."

Dieu, that was more than two hours ago!

"You would make a good policewoman," he remarked. "Always on the stakeout."

"So I've been told."

Was this the game she wanted to play? The cool, calm professional with the mask firmly in place again? He glanced quickly through the window and noticed that she'd placed herself well. She had a clear view of whoever entered Heritage House, as well as the length of the verandah in front of his suite. There was one glaring vulnerability, however.

"I see you have set yourself in an enviable position, but what if someone creeps up behind you?"

She pointed to the large glass window next to her that separated the garden from the open foyer. "I can see them in the reflection."

"Above you?"

"The timber slats along the floor of the balcony are positioned far apart enough to let light through. I'd be able to see, and hear them, walking."

He beckoned to the river, and at the glinting ripples that travelled lazily to the shore, in the wake of one of the many ferries that plied their way up and down the waterway.

She seemed to consider it for a while, staring across the water to the ochre rock cliffs on the other side. Her expression was serious when she faced him, but there was a glint of amusement in her eyes.

"You're right. If somebody was to commandeer a powerboat and lead a team of people in a jet-by shooting, armed with several machine-guns, then I would probably face some difficulty stopping them."

He nodded sagely. "I thought so."

"You could always take my advice and request that Ryan handle bodyguard duty with me," she suggested, tilting her head to one side.

Did she know how attractive she looked like that, with the afternoon sun picking up the highlights in her already fair hair? There was a charm here that she probably didn't even know she had, and Yves wanted to bask in its aura for a while longer.

"Can he halt several men with machine-guns?" he asked with a lifted eyebrow.

"He'd give it a damn good try."

Yves detected the seriousness under her jest and shook his head. "I feel safe enough around you, ma petite. I don't need Ryan Greenwood's added presence."

"And you still want me at tonight's dinner?" He must have looked blankly at her, because she continued in a rush. "It's just that it's a celebration dinner for your business deal. I don't mind. I mean, I'll follow you, but I don't have to be included in the meal. I can wait somewhere for you."

Yves felt a deep frown form on his face. "And how would that look if I deliberately left out a member of my team?" he asked, indignant. How could she even think of such crassness from him?

"But I'm not—"

"You are working for me, are you not?" he interrupted.

"Yes, but—"

"And you have duties to perform?"

"Yes, but—"

"And I am the person paying you, mais non?"

"Yes," she replied in that short, irritated tone he was beginning to like very much from her.

He shrugged. "Leaving you out of the celebration dinner would be like leaving Guy out. It is unforgivable, for many reasons. It would also show a lack of respect to Monsieur Nelson."

"Well, I wouldn't want to disappoint Mr. Nelson," she agreed weakly.

"D'accord. Then you will accompany us, and I will hear no more of this nonsense of waiting for me in some dark corner, starving all night while I enjoy the best seafood your country has to offer." He paused, and tried to sound innocent rather than sly. "Does your country have good seafood?"

"Oh yes," Helen confirmed happily. "Crabs, oysters, Moreton Bay bugs."

Distracted, she started describing the ocean up and down the Queensland coast, and the variety of seafood that could be caught in those warm waters. Yves let a small smile curve his lips. It was done. She would be attending. Suddenly he felt a lot better.

* * * *

Helen thought she had packed enough in her small case to last her through bodyguard duty for a week, but she was swiftly running out of clothes choices. She thought she would be blending into the background not being scrutinised by two fashion-conscious European men. Every time she met Yves, she saw the assessment in his gaze and wondered if she was disappointing his aesthetic sense completely with her taste in clothes.

The problem was she didn't really have anything suitable to wear to a celebratory business dinner with multi-millionaires – if not billionaires, as in Yves' case. Desperate, she pulled out a tunic from the wardrobe that faintly resembled a pirate shirt, with a lace-up v-necked collar and puffy long sleeves. What had even possessed her to buy something like that? She must have been with Sue while cruising one of the many arts fairs that popped up regularly along the banks of the river, and suffering temporary insanity. But, she admitted as she flicked it back and forth, it looked jazzy enough, covered with a muted paisley pattern, and she could wear it with her serviceable trousers and still look reasonably dressy. She could have slipped back into the flapper dress she had worn to dinner with Yves—she knew she looked good in it, and it fitted her like a second skin—but she didn't want to stand out. There was enough on her mind without adding the disturbing and intense looks from a particular Frenchman to the mix. In fact, the day was going so well, she didn't want to think about anything difficult at all. She had focused on her work, made sure the environment was safe for her clients, exchanged pleasantries with their driver for the day, and spent a pleasant afternoon in the sun, watching the river traffic and listening to the muted sounds of traffic on the freeway behind her. When she wasn't stuck in it herself, the sounds of vehicles moving along a road could be almost hypnotic.

After speaking with her for an hour—it always surprised her that a man like him would be happy just to talk about nothing special for such a long time—Yves had retreated to his suite to get ready for dinner, and she did the same. Right now, she was putting the finishing touches to her gypsy-style outfit, adding some muted gold studs to her ears, brushing her hair back, and quickly applying make-up.

At six forty-five, their driver, Tom — Mick had finished his shift for the day — drove them to the mall, letting them out as close as possible to the restaurant.

"It's difficult finding a park around here," he told them as they left the car. The men frowned, but Helen knew he meant a parking spot rather than a large square of greenery, and nodded. "I'll be close by, but call me five minutes before you need me, and I'll meet you back here."

He sped away with a wave.

The pedestrian mall was one of the most popular stretches of walkway in the city. Muted, rectangular grey pavers lined the street, turning the area into a wide boulevard, punctuated every now and then by a cafe/restaurant, performing busker, or occasional shady tree. Even though it was relatively early in the evening, crowds were beginning to form, couples, groups and singles casually strolling, and pondering on the food choices open to them.

Helen moved Yves and Guy through the crowd, alert to any change in the pattern of crowd behaviour, the presage of another imminent attack, but all movement was benevolent. And nobody was looking at them suspiciously.

They had argued with her in disbelief, but she was firm in convincing them that dinner wear in Brisbane did not necessarily mean a jacket and tie. In fact, she told them, Scott might somehow think they were unable to relax if they turned up to dinner in the same kind of clothes as they'd conducted their business meeting in earlier that day. Shepherding her charges to the restaurant, Helen was glad they had eventually taken her advice. The open-necked shirts, folded at the cuffs, and casual trousers that both men wore blended well into the crowd. As long as they didn't say anything, it was unlikely they would draw attention to themselves. As if aware of her silent wishes, both Yves and Guy were quiet, letting her lead the way up the mall, stopping only when they reached a discreet set of stairs leading upwards, next to a brass plaque.

'Roy's' was a simple name for one of the best known restaurants in the region. They ascended the carpeted steps that opened into a cosy bar area, decorated heavily in dark timber. Near one end of the bar, a lectern marked the boundary to the restaurant. Helen had a quick look into the dining area and saw Scott and Ian already seated there, waving when they caught sight of her. With a nod, she asked Yves and Guy to precede her to the table.

The welcomes were warm and sincere all around and although Helen couldn't sit where she wanted — Scott had already commandeered the position with the clearest view to the door — she made do by sitting next to him. Yves sat on the other side, where he could watch her over dinner. She pretended not to notice.

She refused a glass of the wonderfully expensive chablis that Scott ordered, prompting him to ask her if she was somehow uncomfortable or feeling unwell.

"I'm sorry I didn't have time to ask before," he remarked to her, "but do you work for Yves? It's just that I thought I heard a dinky-di Aussie accent there."

Helen laughed, and felt Yves' gaze narrow in on her. "I was born and raised in Brisbane," she replied. "But I am working with Mr. de Saint Nerin during his Australian visit."

"Oh?" Scott's sharp gaze was openly curious.

She couldn't tell him she was his bodyguard. But the only other term she could use — security escort — tended to make people forget the first word and only concentrate on the second, and she didn't think Yves would appreciate being associated with such a label.

"I'm his liaison," she said in a burst of inspiration. "Because neither of the gentlemen," she indicated Yves and Guy, "have been to this country before, they contacted my employers. I was hired to act as a gopher for them should they require any local information or resources."

Scott considered her reply for a second, then nodded. "Fair enough. I'll probably be doing the same thing when I visit them in Paris," he joked. "But does that mean you can't have even one glass of wine with us? After all, we're celebrating the beginning of an international partnership."

Now that she had dug herself into this hole, Helen found she had to dig a little deeper. She put a hand to her forehead. "I have a bit of a headache," she explained in a low voice. "I'd love a glass of wine, but I don't think my head will thank me."

He patted her other hand as it rested on the table. "Good lass. I understand completely." He turned to talk to Ian and Helen looked over at Yves. He was grateful for her fibs, she could tell that much, and she couldn't help but smile at him. Wasn't it part of her job after all to protect her client? If Yves wanted, some time later on, to explain to Scott about Leonid Alexandrov then he was free to do so, but the Australian wouldn't hear it from her.

Scott rose to the festive nature of the occasion by ordering such platters of seafood that there was hardly any room left on the table for their wine glasses and cutlery. As the five of them worked their way through plump oysters, oversized prawns, succulent crab and tender fillets of fish, staff efficiently whisked away bowls of seafood feast remainders—shells, claws and bones—replacing them with clean containers ready for the next culinary attack. Helen ate sparingly, but still more than she was used to. Three bottles of wine had been consumed in total, and she shuddered to think how much she had contributed to the lessening of the marine population with her own restrained greed.

But no matter how much food had been demolished, there was still room for a cheese board and accompanying port at the end of the meal. It was close to eleven o'clock when Yves finally decided that they had better call it a night. He haggled, and graciously lost to Scott, the payment of the bill, threatening revenge by taking his two latest business partners to a famous Michelin-starred establishment on the outskirts of Paris when they reciprocated with a visit of their own to France.

Helen imagined the restaurant as the farewell ritual began. It would probably be a renovated farmhouse, maybe even off an unsealed road, fenced by dry stone walls, and drenched in sun and red poppies. The windows would be bevelled glass, the door solid timber, and the smells from the kitchen, absolutely divine. It didn't hurt to imagine such a place, and Helen didn't care if she was woefully mistaken about any of it, because she knew she would never make that trip. In a handful of days, Yves would go back to his life in France, while she would set up her business in Byron Bay. An ache started deep in her chest at that thought, but she thrust it to one side, not willing to spend more time on why she should feel so depressed at the end of a pleasant evening.

The final farewells were said in the mall, beyond the stairs and discreet, darkly painted door.

"I'll see you next Wednesday," Scott boomed, taking Yves' hand and shaking it vigorously. He did the same with Guy's. Ian, now that he seemed used to their presence, also brightened up and said some words that hovered dangerously close to sociability. Helen found him endearing in a geekish way, obviously a man of genius-level intelligence but still socially inept.

Helen waited until they started walking away before she called Tom on her mobile. He promised to be at their rendezvous point in minutes, and they began walking back down the pedestrian mall.

It was a week night, and so the crowds had thinned considerably from their earlier crush. Both Yves and Guy were walking a little slower than on their way to the restaurant. They were both probably too full to amble at a faster pace, she thought with amusement.

They moved off the mall, down a street, and Helen thought she saw the back of the limo waiting for them around the corner, twenty metres away.

And then, for the second time, violence exploded around them.

Chapter Nine

It was difficult to describe, but this attack had a different feel to it. It was more chaotic, less organised. Helen was glad of that, because there were three of them, and they had the element of surprise on their side.

Roughly, they pushed and pulled Yves, Guy and herself into the deep recess of a shopfront and tried to pummel them into unconsciousness. After the initial panic of feeling an arm around her neck subsided, Helen went with the flow, not only allowing herself to be dragged backwards, but actively pushing herself back. She estimated the distance to the closest wall, but was a little off in her calculation, and the jar that hit her attacker also vibrated through her. She took advantage of the slight lessening of pressure at her throat, to elbow him in the ribs. He was tall and broad, of solid build. With a gasp, he let go and Helen twirled, bringing his head down to her knee in a vicious strike then slamming it, face-first, into the wall. She heard the scuffles from the other two attackers and was in no mood to be delicate. She slammed her attacker's head twice more into the wall, and was already moving away while he was still sliding to the ground.

The night time shadows made it difficult to make out exactly where one person ended and another began, but it was enough to know that a second attacker had his back to her. Helen punched him, hard, in each kidney, and threw him backwards as he fell, in a more ruthless repeat of what she had done to Yves a lifetime ago in the carpeted room at Heritage House. It was only when he was down that she realised she had just despatched Guy's attacker. The third of the group was quick to join his fellows, following a wet thud that Helen correctly surmised was the sound of Yves' fist meeting an unsuspecting jaw.

Without a word, she grabbed the sleeves of both Frenchmen, and ushered them out of the building's shadowed darkness and back down the street. She didn't speak until they were in the car and Tom, after one startled glance, jammed down the accelerator and sped them away.

"We don't have much time," she told them hurriedly. "When Tom stops, I want both of you to get into Heritage House and prepare overnight bags. Take only the essentials. I'll be back in fifteen minutes."

"Where are you going?" Yves asked sharply.

Helen ignored him. "I will give two short beeps of the horn. When you hear that, come out and head straight for my car. It'll be a white sedan."

The limo was already cruising down the city street closest to the river. Helen knew she had less than a minute of briefing time left.

"If there's anybody waiting for you, if anyone attacks you," she swallowed, "call the police as soon as you can. If you can't get to a phone, scream, throw things, make as much noise as possible in order to draw attention to yourself." The limo pulled up outside the welcoming lights of their rented residence. "Go. Now."

To their credit, both men—even Yves—were adept at following orders once the need arose. Helen should have directed Tom to keep driving once the door closed behind them, but she couldn't do it. She waited until she saw lights go on, yellow and muted, in Yves' suite then, a few moments later, upstairs where Guy must be staying. She waited, straining her ears, but heard no soft sounds of a fight or screams for help. Damn the man! If Yves had only taken her advice and hired two bodyguards, she wouldn't find herself in such a quandry, having to make the tough decision of wasting time in order to check out the security of the house, instead of using that time to organise their getaway.

Finally, after a handful more of precious minutes ticked by, Helen told Tom to head for Fortitude Valley. She wasn't going to make the mistake of going to her apartment. For all she knew, Alexandrov might know who she was and had her place watched. But one of the things that made the Valley an inconvenient place to live also added to her security. In the crowded inner-city suburb, she didn't have the luxury of a garage beneath her apartment, so Helen's car was parked a distance away. She directed Tom to drop her off at the top of Brunswick Street, on the edge of the Chinatown district, and waved him off after a quick word that she'd be in touch, but not for several more days.

After watching the red lights of the sedan disappear into the traffic, Helen took a quick look around, and crossed the road. This part of the city was run down and faintly menacing, but its denizens seemed to somehow recognise who belonged in their territory and who didn't. Helen, confident but watchful, strode down the street to the brightly lit, multi-level car-park halfway up the block. There were no footsteps behind her and no figures loitering in front of her. It seemed she was safe for the time being.

The car-park had an elevator, but Helen, still keyed up from the fight and distrustful, took the stairs, bounding up them two at a time. She didn't draw attention to herself by running across the concrete of the second level but walked swiftly, keeping her eyes straight, alert to any peripheral sound and movement. It was almost midnight and it appeared that, except for the two staff at the booth on the ground level, the building was entirely deserted.

She walked over to her car, a white, Japanese four-door sedan. It looked ordinary, but was overpowered — just the way she liked it. She unlocked it from a distance, slipped into the driver's seat and paused. Every criminal movie she had ever seen ran through her head, a litany of potential disasters. Car chases. Deliberately punctured tyres. A car bomb.

The last one resonated the most, and her fingers trembled as she inserted the key into

the car's ignition. She took a deep breath, turned the key with a quick jerk. And exhaled in relief as the engine throbbed to life.

She reversed out of her reserved car bay, exited the car-park and headed back to the city. The urge to analyse the messy details of the last half-hour was strong, but that would only fritter away her concentration. It was bad enough that, in the ten minutes it took to reach Heritage House again, a whole parade of nightmare scenarios crowded into her head.

What if there were two teams of attackers? What if the second team had already attacked the house and done their job? She imagined Yves on the floor and bleeding, his eyes staring blindly at the ceiling. Her grip on the steering wheel tightened.

No! She wouldn't think of such things. But the images refused to go away, and Helen felt herself consumed by fear. Fear? That was a shallow word for the panic that seized her. A thick band of cold steel coiled itself around her chest, tightening its grip, making it difficult to breathe. She opened her mouth and took hurried gasps into her lungs to try and break the feeling of suffocation, but it only helped a little. Her hands, knuckles white as they clenched the driving controls, were as chilled as ice, yet slippery with sweat. With every turn and gear change, she thought she'd lose control of the vehicle and plunge it into a building or send it careening across a deserted city street.

If anything happened to Yves, she didn't know how she would live with herself afterwards. It wasn't just that he was her responsibility for as long as he was on Australian soil. And it wasn't the money. She slammed to a halt at a pair of red traffic lights at the same time as the truth hit her. Could it be true? Could she be in love with Yves de Saint Nerin?

She let go of the steering wheel with her right hand and hit it a couple of times. No, no, no! What kind of fool was she to do a stupid thing like that? In love with a client, who happened to be one of the richest men in Europe? On a scale of one to ten for stupidity, this certainly rated a few thousand!

The lights turned green. Helen jerked the gear stick into first and continued driving. When had it happened? When she'd thought of him, broken and bleeding, back at Heritage House? When she'd demonstrated her expertise on him, keeping as close to him as a lover even as she pounded lightly into him? Or when she'd first caught sight of him, standing nonchalantly off to one side, on her first visit to Heritage House?

Whenever it had happened, it was idiocy on a level she had only previously dreamed about. In less than two weeks, assuming he was alive—Helen pressed more heavily on the accelerator pedal at the thought— he would be safely back in France, dining at those Michelin restaurants he'd told Scott about, and no doubt getting ready to escort the next incomparably beautiful model or member of European nobility to some glittering event.

She was Helen Collier, reasonably good-looking, reasonably successful, but nonetheless, a woman who worked for a living. She had no business even considering a relationship with someone like Yves.

The car slowed to a stop just outside Heritage House, and Helen beeped the horn twice, softly. At first, nothing seemed to happen—oh no! He's dead!

The breath caught in her throat and refused to let go, cutting off passage so she couldn't even swallow past it. Then the front door opened, and two figures strode purposefully down the footpath, each bearing a small piece of luggage. Yves got in the front, passing his bag back to Guy to rest on the seat next to him. Helen pulled away from the curb before both doors had slammed shut.

They had enough sense to keep quiet as she negotiated her way onto the freeway, heading south. It was only when they had cleared the inner city completely, whizzing past dark suburbs lit only by the regular white glow of street lights, that they spoke.

"Who were those men?" Guy asked.

"I don't know," Helen replied, "but I'm not taking any chances."

"You think they're from Alexandrov," Yves stated.

Yes, that had been her first thought, but there was still much about the incident that didn't make sense to her. She checked her rear view mirror, noticing some distant pairs of headlights behind them. Hopefully, they would drop to nothing as she continued the drive.

"I'm really not sure, but we're not hanging around to find out."

She reached for her mobile and tapped out a number she knew in her sleep. It answered on the third ring.

"Ryan, we're on the move," she said before he could bark out a greeting.

"You got jumped again?"

"Three men. Nobody hurt on our side. I'm on the way to the safe house."

"Where did they jump you?"

She gave him detailed instructions of the corner near which they were ambushed.

"I'll call only if it's urgent," he told her. "If I don't, contact me in a few days." And he terminated the call.

"Where are we going?" Yves asked.

"To a safe house. Did you wrap up affairs at Heritage House?"

"I left instructions with the staff to continue as normal, but told them Guy and I were going on a short trip and didn't know when we would be back."

She nodded. "That's probably safest."

Could he feel the tense thrumming of her body as she drove southwards? He must have. They seemed to be attuned to each other's bodies, whether they liked it or not. Correction, whether she liked it or not.

"Where is this safe house?" he asked, after another silence of ten minutes.

"Somewhere safe." Only her tone belied the flippant words.

"Is it far away?"

She glanced quickly at the clock on the dashboard. It was twelve thirty-five in the morning. "Another two hours, maybe a bit more."

"Quite a way out of Brisbane."

"Yes it is."

There was only one place Helen could think of that she regarded as remotely secure, and that was her parents' house—no, it was her house now—at Byron Bay. Ryan knew about it, but even he didn't know exactly where it was. It would be after two in the morning by the time she reached it, and she would be exhausted. Already, she felt the tiredness creep up on her, as the adrenaline washed out of her system. She knew she would be asleep before her head even touched the pillow.

The outskirts of Brisbane flashed past, and they were in that nebulous area between cities, the highway bounded by large acreage properties, one or two rooms illuminated by lights that remained on long into the early morning hours. What little traffic there was behind her had disappeared completely. In the back, Helen heard heavy, steady breathing and knew Guy had fallen asleep. But Yves remained awake and alert beside her.

"How long will we be staying at this safe house?" Yves voice broke the silence. It was good having him around as he stopped her from falling asleep with his disturbing presence and questions that demanded answers.

"As far as I'm concerned, until you fly back to France." There was a bitter-sweet quality to the thought—to have him all to herself, until she lost him to his home country.

" C'est impossible." His answer was quick and direct. "At the very least, I have to be back in Brisbane next week to sign the initial agreement with Scott Nelson."

She gave him as long a look as she dared before turning her attention back to the road. She didn't have to say a word. Yves knew exactly what she was thinking.

"Alexandrov has already affected my business, my family, myself, far more than I like or am comfortable with," he explained. "I have to make a stand."

"And get yourself killed in the process?" She said it lightly, with coolness, to hide the clench of her stomach as she conjured up images to match her words.

"Both times we were attacked, they were nothing but thugs. Perhaps the attackers tonight were a little more skilled, but the chance of me getting killed is remote at best."

Did he really believe that? How could he be so frivolous about his life? Even a lucky punch could knock him out and send him tumbling over a balcony...or a drunken tackle could smash the back of his skull against a kerb.

"Pete," she whispered softly, staring straight ahead.

"I'm sorry, did you say something?"

"I'm just thinking how foolish you are," Helen told him bitterly. "Maybe you think it's your money that keeps you invulnerable, but you can lose your life in a heartbeat and not know it. A life's worth of potential gone in the blink of an eye, and not a thing you can do about it. You're dead, but the people who cared for you are still alive, wondering how the hell it happened and wishing they could somehow turn back the clock."

She tried to keep her tone as impersonal as possible—even though she knew that was no way to talk to a client, and certainly no way to talk to a man like Yves—but knew she failed. Their assaults, following so closely after Pete's death, was too much pain to ignore. Maybe it was a good thing that she was burying herself at Byron Bay and giving up the potential for lucrative bodyguard contracts like this one. At this point in life, after losing such a close friend, she didn't think she was tough enough to continue in the profession. She would stick to teaching children how to finesse their kicks and to helping adults keep up their fitness, and leave the life and death decisions of someone involved in personal security behind her forever.

"Was he a good friend?"

Helen's hand jerked on the wheel. It wasn't much, but it was enough to send the car jolting close up to the lane boundary for a moment before she corrected the action. It was enough to tell Yves that he'd scored a direct hit.

"Yes, he was," she finally said when he didn't break the silence. "He was a good instructor and a great human being."

"Did you love him?"

How should she answer that? That, once, she'd thought she did? Or that she'd felt, with time and a deepening relationship between the two of them, she would have grown to love him? How could she talk about her lessened expectations, considering the profession she had chosen? Of gentle men, too frightened to approach her, and ungentle men who were too ungentle in all things? And then Pete had been there like a warm, solid refuge in a storm. He wasn't afraid of her and didn't have anything to prove. She hadn't gone searching for love, because only those two conditions, confidence and respect?impossibly hard, it seemed, to fulfil?were enough. So, she'd thought Pete was enough and had even started imagining a tentative future that included more than just herself. How wrong she had been!

It wasn't enough that she had lost Pete. Now, when she had only just begun picking up the pieces of her life again, along came Yves de Saint Nerin. Tall, dark, and handsome. Wealthy and charming. As hypnotising as a king cobra fixated on a mouse. And he was so far out of her league, he might as well have come from another planet. Of all the men, in all the situations, in all the places of the world, she thought wryly, shamelessly breaking the quote from a famous movie, why did it have to be him she fell in love with?

And it was love, of that she was sure. There was nothing else that could explain the uneven staccato of her heart whenever she caught sight of him. Or the equally strong urges to run towards him and away from him, at the same time. Maybe if she was in a different situation, a wealthy socialite in her own right, she might be more confident about exploring the attraction that crackled between them, but she was only one of his staff, and a temporary member at that. She couldn't believe how strong the impulse had been to give in to what he offered, to entwine their bodies in mindless pleasure for long stretches of hours, and reality be damned. And, while it had lasted, it had been heaven.

But she also knew that letting her fantasies and actions distract her from her job were putting him in incredible danger. That increased her sense of culpability. Maybe, once he was gone, she could regain her self-respect. She'd be miserable. But she'd be herself again. Surely that was something to cling to?

Her musings took time. In fact they took so many minutes that by the time her thoughts finally circled back to the present, it was too late to answer Yves' question. She knew he would take her silence to mean that yes, she had loved Pete. And she had, as a trusted friend. It would do no harm for Yves to think that there was more to the story than that.

* * * *

She loves him still.

Yves was not a fool. He knew what that long pause, stretching almost to eternity, meant. Whomever she spoke of with the heartbreak still lodged in her throat, whose death she still grieved over, was someone she had loved dearly. He had taken a chance, alluding casually to a man, hoping that she would explain it was a brother or cousin or acquaintance, who had lost his life in such a meaningless fashion. But the stab of pain he'd felt in his chest as he uttered the words deepened with Helen's answer.

He was a good instructor, and a great human being.

Of course. He should have known that she would have fallen in love with someone from her world, someone who protected and taught other people. Whereas he...he had only one real student, only one person he was deliberately training, and that was the young man snoring softly in the back of the car. His greatest gift was the ability to make money, but what benefited others? Expansion of businesses, employment of staff? Also had the result of benefiting himself. In contrast, when Helen shared her skills and expertise, it was all given away, selflessly, with no thought of her own safety.

Against someone else like that, a man she both loved and respected, a rival whose name he did not even know, what chance did he stand?

He looked out the window at the dark smudges of trees, indistinct beyond the bright arc of the freeway lights, and brooded. By thinking of the dead man as a rival, that meant that Yves had already decided to pursue Helen himself. He cast a quick glance her way. And why not? She was like a breath of fresh air to him. She was lively, intelligent and self-confident. He admired the way she was able to take care of herself, even as he wanted to shower her with gifts and tell her that she didn't have to.

But, merde, how did he go about defeating a memory, a ghost? If he could have fought dirty, Yves would have done it without hesitation. After all, he was a man who saw what he wanted and went after it. It wouldn't have pricked his conscience at all to hire a team of investigators to probe the background and dealings of a potential rival...or partner. All was fair in love and business. But what did one do when that man was dead? How could he compete with the hallowed memory of this mysterious fellow instructor and 'great human being' without making himself look like an insensitive idiot in the process? That was if he stood even the slightest chance of success. All he could be sure of was the attraction between him and Helen. But that could be an attraction based only on physical chemistry. At least on Helen's part. She was too well schooled to give away too much with those stormy blue-grey eyes of hers. Maybe the memory of her dead lover still exerted a hold too strong to break? But how could this be, he wondered in sudden bewilderment. Women found him irresistible. Usually.

What he needed, he decided, was more intelligence. He needed to find out exactly who this ghost was from Helen's past. Maybe by getting her to talk about it, it would ease her pain and give him a better insight into her character. There was still much about her that intrigued and puzzled him, and that was in addition to their incandescent combination in bed. It made for a potent mix.

The landscape streamed past in shadowed monotony. Yves felt tired but not enough to fall asleep. Also, he didn't think it right to doze off while Helen still drove. He would have offered to take over the driving of the car, but he didn't know where they were going. If this had been Europe, he wouldn't have hesitated. Besides, she liked being in control and wouldn't relish relinquishing it to his grasp. He had noticed that about her, almost from the first moment he saw her. He had wanted to see a bit more of Australia but not under these conditions, settled next to an attractive but prickly female bodyguard, racing off into the night. He glanced at the clock. They would reach their destination in a little more than two hours, she had said one and a half hours ago. Well, at least they were more than halfway through their journey.

He knew he should be making small talk, keeping her awake on the long drive, but every question that popped into his head somehow, inevitably, snaked back to her dead boyfriend, and that, for now, was a fruitless avenue to explore.

"I've been thinking about that group of three men waiting for us after our dinner with Scott," he finally ventured. There, the hint of an intellectual puzzle should keep her awake. And keep him away from the topic he most wanted to explore.

"So have I," she replied. Her voice was a bit distracted but friendly enough, indicating he had hit just the right topic and tone of delivery with her. Bien.

She frowned at the windscreen. "I've been wondering how they knew where we'd be."

"You don't think they followed us to the restaurant and laid in wait?"

"Maybe," she conceded. "That's the only explanation that makes sense. But why attack us in such a semi-public place? If they had followed us there, wouldn't it have made more sense to have just ambushed us at Heritage House in the first place?"

"There are always one or two staff around the House," he countered.

"Yes, but these were three big guys. And there are more likely to be police near the Mall where we were than close to Heritage House. It seems they chose an awfully risky plan."

"Are you thinking they were not from Alexandrov at all?"

"I don't know what to think," she admitted candidly. "One thing is for sure. I didn't quite expect the assignment to be quite so, exciting."

Yves tightened his lips in sudden guilt. That was his fault, of course. He could have made it easier on her by agreeing to hire a second bodyguard, but he had let his own personal and selfish desires overrule his logic.

"I mean, I know you paid a lot of money," she added in a hurry, obviously misreading his guilty silence for censure. "And I don't mean to imply that I didn't expect to work—"

"You misunderstand," he interrupted. "I am blaming myself. I should have taken your advice and contacted Ryan Greenwood after the first incident. I will never forgive myself for putting a woman like you in harm's way."

How could he live with himself if anything happened to her? Already, he feared that her quirky and amusingly barbed nature had burrowed under his skin. Whatever happened between them, it would be a long time, if ever, before he forgot Helen Collier.

"A—? Sorry, what did you say?"

He stared out the window and didn't really notice the rising edge in her voice.

"It's true," he murmured, idly counting the street lights that whizzed past. "Putting a woman in harm's way? Depending on her to stop a criminal? I think I must have rocks in my head."

"Rocks," she said softly. "Oh yes, I think I agree with that."

It was the silkiness in her tone that finally triggered a degree of alarm in him.

"Pardon?"

"So you think that a woman can't be depended on to stop a criminal? Did I hear that right?"

Yves replayed the words he said in his head and winced at their obvious ambiguity. In truth, he had spoken without thinking too deeply on the interpretation which, he now admitted, could really be badly construed. He must be more tired than he thought.

"You misunderstand."

"I don't think so, Mr. de Saint Nerin."

Ah, she must be upset to say his name thus. Usually, it was "Yves", like a lover's whisper after the tumult of orgasm. He always enjoyed hearing his name from her lips.

"I did not mean to imply that you are somehow," he searched for the appropriate word, "unskilled in the matter of looking after my person. I just meant that this is no job for a woman."

If he was hoping to mollify her, he feared?judging from the set look on her face, formidable, even in profile?that he had just done the equivalent of throwing petrol onto a blazing fire.

"And what would be the correct job for a woman? A mistress perhaps? A maid to follow you around and pick up your things?"

"Mais non," he protested, stifling a yawn. What were they arguing about again? "I'm a very tidy man. I pride myself on being organised."

"You're missing the point."

But he heard the small filament of laughter in her voice. Had he said something funny now? He hadn't thought so, but he was not going to lose such a slim advantage. Wisely, he kept quiet.

"Women don't like being coddled."

"I fear to disagree," he said, imagining exactly how he'd like to coddle her. She wouldn't protest. Purr perhaps, he would bet on it, but he doubted she would protest.

"Well maybe the women in your world like to be coddled," she corrected. "But, in my world, they just put their shoulders to the wheel and keep going."

Ah, he could disagree with her on that count. Delphine, for example, was someone who also worked hard, despite the fact that she managed to look like an ethereal deity while she was doing it. But he wasn't going to bring any women of his acquaintance into this discussion. That would certainly take the conversation in a direction he didn't want it to go.

"I don't believe you," he said softly.

She shot him a quick look of disbelief. "It's true. I don't expect anyone to treat me as less than his equal."

"That's something different. Equal. Coddle. They are two separate arguments. I respect your abilities as a fighter and a bodyguard. But I could also spoil you. The two are not mutually exclusive." He paused, and knew she didn't believe him. She shifted in her seat, stretching her back a little and that gave him an idea.

"When was the last time you were given a shoulder massage?" he asked.

"A shoulder massage?" She snaked him a wary look.

"Oui. Last month? Last year?"

"I...last year, I suppose."

"Your boyfriend? He did this for you?"

She hesitated. "Er...yes."

"Did you feel that he was somehow trying to rob you of your independence by doing such a thing?"

"No, of course not." She snorted then her face cleared. "It's not the same thing."

"But of course it is." He leant forward, closer to her. "If I chose to indulge you, that would not mean I didn't respect you."

He was so intent on the changing expressions on her face that he didn't realise they had been travelling along an inclined driveway. The ground levelled out and, with an audible sigh of relief, Helen pulled on the hand brake and switched off the engine.

"We're here," she said. "Welcome to the safe house."

Chapter Ten

Helen had never been so happy to reach the Byron house before. Without waiting for a response, she quickly stepped out of the car, the slam of the closing door jolting Guy, still asleep in the back, awake. She heard the scuffle of their bags then both sets of doors on the passenger side opened.

Not waiting for them, she walked up the short pathway to the verandah then paused. The moon was hidden behind clouds so the outline of the house was indistinct, but the sound of waves crashing on the beach below was like music to her ears. Helen took a breath of the sea-kissed air and felt herself relax. Coming to her parents' house at Byron always affected her like this. It was a refuge for her away from the crowds and pressures of her other life.

She jiggled the keys in her hand, found the right one and slipped it into the lock. The air inside was a little musty—it had been more than two months since she last visited—but inviting, as if the love between her parents, the happy holidays the whole family had spent here, had soaked into the wood, the very foundations of the house itself. It reached out, enveloping her, and Helen couldn't help the smile that curved her lips as she stepped forward, past the sun room and small living room, to switch on the light in the corridor that led to two bedrooms, divided by a single bathroom.

"There are two beds in that bedroom," she told the two men, who followed close behind her, indicating the room at the back of the house. "Feel free to make yourselves at home. I'll see you in the morning."

She turned and walked back to the kitchen, switching on the light and glancing quickly at the wall clock that ticked quietly away next to the refrigerator. It was two-thirty in the morning, and she felt a strange mixture of excitement and exhaustion. In an attempt to calm her nerves, she opened the fridge door and grimaced, knowing she wouldn't find anything useful there, but just checking anyway. Grocery shopping was obviously going to be the first thing on her list for the morning, especially with two adult males in the house.

She heard a noise behind her and knew, even as she turned around, that it was Yves. He looked tired but still irresistibly handsome, his dark hair a bit tousled, and his shirt rumpled. She realised she hadn't given either man enough time to clean up or get changed after their assault in the mall. Just barked orders at them then drove them interstate to the safest place she could think of. Her eyes moved down his shirt and to his right hand, which was bruised and crusted with rusty flecks of dried blood.

With a gasp, she hurried forward. "When did that happen?"

He looked down, as if he had forgotten about the injury. "When we were attacked. I think I must have hit my attacker a few times, although I don't quite remember it."

She led him to the sink and put his hand under the tap, letting cool water run over it. "That must hurt."

With his free hand, he turned her hands over. "You don't have such marks."

"No. I don't really hit people that way."

"Oh."

A grin quirked Helen's lips. He didn't really understand what she was saying, but that was all right. After all, he wasn't the one being paid money to keep someone else safe.

Yves looked around as he let the water soothe his bruising. "Where are we? Is this place yours?"

"It used to be my parents' place." She switched off the tap then grabbed a tea towel and gently patted his hand dry. "But it's mine now."

"And we're south of Brisbane?"

"Actually, we're in another state. We're in New South Wales, just on the outskirts of the town of Byron Bay."

"I see."

"We'll be safe here," she assured him. "Not even Ryan knows exactly where this house is."

He took the towel from her and finished drying his hands then threw it casually onto the kitchen counter top. His eyes, looking shadowed and impenetrable under the cool fluorescent lighting, never left her, and Helen swallowed nervously. This was why she had felt that strange frisson of excitement when they entered the house. Because she knew that she would be forced to keep close to Yves for the next week, until he got back on that flight to France. Close enough to feel the heat from his skin and to breathe in the masculine scent of him. The house was superbly situated on one of the coastal bluffs overlooking the sea, but it was small, and there wasn't much room to avoid another person. The animal part of her knew that, and revelled in the fact that she would be close to the man she'd fallen in love with.

The revelation made her thunderstruck. Was it true? Did she love Yves? She looked up into his handsome features and moved away, slipping sideways past him in one economical movement.

Yes.

What she'd feared in the car, on her drive to Heritage House, was unfortunately correct. Yves was safe, but the pounding of her heart had still not subsided. It was irrational. She had not gone looking for it, content to continue quietly grieving for Pete, but it had come crashing down on her head. Love. And only with one of the most unattainable men on the planet.

Misery kept Helen's feet moving as she avoided Yves, stepping into the small living room that served as her study. A desk was pushed up against the window, overlooking the overgrown garden at the side of the house. When she finally moved down here that would be something else she'd have to take care of.

"There's internet access," she told him a little breathlessly. He moved silently, following her, tracking her footfalls. "If you need to check anything."

The recognition of her feelings was too raw, too immediate. She had to get away. Flashing him a quick grin while looking just over his shoulder, she moved to the corridor. "It's really late, so I'll say goodnight."

"Shall I switch off the lights in the house then?" he asked, his voice mocking. He knew that she was avoiding him yet again, but not why. Oh, please God, not why!,

"Yes, thank you."

She was past embarrassment. She fled to her room and closed the door quietly behind her. Not even daring to switch on the light, she leaned back against the timber and closed her eyes as she tried to steady her breathing.

In love.

Now that she knew what it felt like, she wanted no part of it. It seared her, burning away the logic she had always prided herself on. It made her put every rational thought to one side, wondering only whether Yves was all right, whether he could love her, whether the trembling wish for a future together was mere fantasy. Why couldn't it be someone more accessible that she felt this yearning for? One of Ryan's group of competent and likeable instructors or a charming man she might bump into while shopping at Chinatown? Why did it have to be a super-rich European businessman, who had flown to Australia on a flying visit? A one-off event caused more by the machinations of a criminal than any genuine curiosity on Yves' side.

Helen knocked her head against the door then stopped, in case Yves heard the thumping and wondered about its source.

The only way she could consider even beginning a relationship with Yves was if he was out of danger. She knew he was interested in her, those intense gazes of his burned through her clothing and caused her skin to combust. And the sex between them was dynamite. But it was the wrong thing, at the wrong place, in the wrong time. So where did that leave her?

Helen moved across the room, slowly peeling off her clothes and finding a pair of pyjamas by touch in the dresser drawer. She kept the curtains drawn, knowing the strong morning light would slant through and wake her up in any case. It was almost three o'clock in the morning, and it felt like it, the burden of the preceding hours weighing heavily on her shoulders.

Exhausted, Helen collapsed onto the bed, not even pulling the bedspread down first, and instantly fell asleep.

* * * *

Helen woke to a phone call on her mobile. She glanced at the bedside clock and groaned. She had been asleep for a little more than three and a half hours. Still, she reached for her small phone—she would have to charge it that day with the spare lead she always kept at the house—and pressed the green button.

"Hel, it's Ryan. Call me."

The sound of Ryan's voice was enough to snap her to wakefulness. Not even bothering with a reply, he terminated the call. A part of her wondered how much of Ryan's command was his desire to play at spies. Then again, in his line of work, one couldn't be too sure.

Still yawning, Helen padded out to the phone in the living room, using the land line to call her old instructor. He picked up the call before the second ring began.

"I've got some good news for you," he started, without preamble. "Those thugs at the mall weren't Alexandrov's men."

"What?" Helen frowned at the receiver.

"After I spoke to you, I got down there with a couple of the lads and started asking questions."

Despite the early hour, Helen couldn't help the grin that split her face. She was sorry she hadn't been around to see that, a vengeful Ryan mercilessly questioning all the denizens of the shadowy, not quite legal environment around Queen Street. The police force had lost a tenacious recruit when Ryan Greenwood had decided to take up martial arts instead of law enforcement.

"And?"

"They were a new gang, up from the south. The usual crowd were only too happy to turn them in, considering they were encroaching on their territory."

"They were blow ins?" Helen asked, surprised. She used the slang for strangers in town.

"Looks like it. We had a bit of a 'talk' with them, and they should already be on their way home by now."

"Did they hurt anyone else?" She had to know.

"No. You were the first. And last. You gave them a good run for their money, Hel. I had a look at them more closely before we sent them packing. They'll not be forgetting Brisbane hospitality in a hurry."

"Yves helped too."

"The Frenchie? He can fight?"

"Didn't do a bad job," Helen remarked, a smile in her voice. Then she sobered. "So you're saying it was complete chance that that gang ran into us?"

"Seems like it."

"And it had nothing to do with Alexandrov?" Helen didn't care that she sounded like a moron. She had to make sure she had the facts right in her head.

"No."

She almost started dancing on the spot. It had been nothing but an episode of bad luck. Yves was safe after all! "So we can return to Brisbane then?"

"I don't know that I'd be in such a rush, if I were you." Ryan's voice was slow, and it was obvious he was thinking as he spoke. "I think I know roughly where you are, and it's where Alexandrov can't easily find you. If you were back in Brisbane, that would give him time to watch you and your movements. Right now, he'll be planning in a vacuum. Do you even need to come back here?"

Helen sobered. "There's a business meeting set for next week. And I'm told," she added ruefully, "that it's critical for Yves to attend."

Ryan sighed. "That's always the way with these rich business types." The pause after his statement was pregnant with meaning, and Helen's fingers tightened on the receiver. "They don't care about much, except making money. You know that, don't you?"

Had she given herself away so transparently? That was Helen's first thought. Ryan had the reputation of being able to pluck facts from the thin air, which was ridiculous. So what had she done or said that made him issue that warning?

She didn't reply to the question.

"Is it going to be a problem keeping them there?" he continued after the extended silence.

"No."

"Then that would be my recommendation. Lay low for the next few days and give me time to nose around. I may turn up something interesting. Can you keep your two occupied till you need to return?"

Helen blushed. "I, I'll have a think about what to do." She willed her mind not to wander off in a well-anticipated direction. "I'll let you know when we're ready to drive back into Brisbane."

"I'll have someone else ready as your back-up when you arrive," he assured her.

"Thanks, Ryan."

"If you need to talk." The older man cleared his throat gruffly. "You know, if there's anything you need me to do, call me."

"Sure. Thanks."

She rested the phone quietly back in its cradle.

Nothing to do with Alexandrov! The words danced her in her head, making her...what? Want to jump into bed with Yves with gleeful abandon? Ryan told her he had sent a gang of three opportunists packing, and all she could do was think of how that would affect her sexual relationship with Yves! Her mind was truly twisted.

She stilled for a moment, listening for noise, but there was none, not even Yves' quiet padding into the room. Quickly, before she had time to rethink, Helen slipped back into her room, hastily throwing on a tank top and jogging pants. After doing up a trusted pair of sneakers, she let herself out the front door. Unless Leonid Alexandrov had several geostationary satellites available for his surveillance use, she was sure Guy and Yves were quite safe, by themselves, in the house.

It wasn't Alexandrov, she thought with a grin. It wasn't him!

Fingers of dawn were lightening into a clear morning over the horizon when Helen bounded down the tall wooden staircase that led from the house to the beach. The timber was grey and weathered but still solid, broken every so often by a small platform where climbers could stop to catch their breath and look out over the Pacific Ocean. This was Byron Bay, the easternmost point of Australia, and there was nothing between Helen and South America but a few islands and the vastness of the ocean.

She breathed in deep of the tangy air, stretching out her arms at the same time, and disturbed a flock of seagulls already awake and pecking at the tiny crabs that called the area between the tide lines their home. Helen walked to the stretch of damp sand, a surer platform for her running, then took off down the beach, her burst of happiness lending wings to her feet.

This was one thing that made coming back to Byron so special. There was really nowhere in Brisbane where she could enjoy such isolation and peace. In front of her, the beach curved gently around several coves, all sheltered and quiet. It was easy to get out of shape in the city, but once she had settled in Byron, she could see these morning jogs becoming a special and permanent part of her day. The sand lightened from a grey to a sparkling white as the sun cleared the watery horizon. Helen ran, stretching her legs and taking deep breaths as she huffed along the sand. Two kilometres down from the timber staircase, the cliffs dipped down until they became sand dunes, and a town emerged from the surrounding hills.

Remembering the need for groceries, Helen headed up Main Beach, walking past the tall pine trees until she reached grass and the road. Already, the sun's rays were warming her back as she walked into the town centre. It was going to be another warm day.

The small supermarket she frequented was closed, but the lights were on, indicating somebody was already at work. With a thoughtful frown on her face, Helen walked up to one of the plate glass windows, waving frantically as she saw the owner, Bill Cook, checking one of the cereal box displays. He turned at the movement outside and smiled widely at her, hurrying to open the staff entrance door.

Bill was a slight, dapper man in his mid-forties, who had been born in Adelaide but had holidayed with his family at Byron Bay in his youth. That one trip had been enough to fire his imagination he told Helen, and, after a string of jobs, he decided, in his early thirties, to move to Byron Bay permanently and try his luck. In his case, it had worked out. He landed the job of assistant manager at the supermarket, met and married a wonderful woman by the name of Gloria, and had three children still attending the local school. He was content with his life, and it showed.

"Hel, are you back in town?" he greeted, stating the obvious. "When did you get in?"

"Hi Bill. Late last night."

He ushered her inside and locked the door behind her. "Are you staying long?"

"A week. I've got a couple of visitors with me," she added carefully. "Some tourist friends down from Brisbane."

"Well, Byron's a great place to bring them." Bill beamed with pride. "I'm sure they'll like it here."

Helen wondered how to keep a lid on the grapevine and decided to stick as close to the truth as possible. "They're rather well known," she added, lowering her voice even though there was nobody around. "There could be photographers asking after them. I'd appreciate it if you kept mum about them being around."

"Flying in those circles now, are you?" he replied, winking. "No worries. Nobody'll hear it from me. And I'll make sure Gloria keeps her trap shut, too."

Helen shrugged. "With avoiding people, I didn't have time to get any groceries in." She petered out, hopefully, and Bill laughed at the expression on her face.

"You'd starve without me, Helen Collier! Go on, get whatever you want. You can square up with me next time you're in town."

"Are you sure?"

"What are you going to do? Lift up that house and drive somewhere else? I know where you are. Besides, it doesn't look like you've got a wallet in those sporty pants of yours."

She pecked him quickly on the cheek and did a quick flit up and down the aisles, taking just enough food for breakfast and lunch. Bill packed everything for her in carry bags and, after being assured that she was fine for the walk home, waved her good-bye from the door of the supermarket.

It took more than half an hour to walk home, but that didn't bother Helen. Life moved at a different pace than in the city, and although she kept a brisk pace, she was happy to be strolling rather than taking Bill up on his offer of a lift.

She was so caught up in the serenity of the morning that she didn't realise anything was amiss until she was walking up the driveway to her house. While still a few metres away, the door flung open with a bang, and Yves emerged, his expression dark and angry. His hair was spiky and unkempt, as if he had run his fingers through it several times, and he was in a pair of striped pyjamas. He must have thrown on the top hurriedly, however, because only one of its buttons was done up. His brown feet were bare.

"Merde! Where have you been?" he demanded. "I wake up and you're gone."

He was obviously flustered, and Helen noticed his accent was a bit more pronounced than usual, as if he was concentrating all his energy on his anger. "Anything could have happened. You leave no note, no sign. I–Guy and I have been frantic. We are stuck here in...in..." He gestured expansively. "Wherever this place is that nobody knows about, and the only link we have is missing. Believe me, cherie, this is not pleasant to wake up to."

Helen heard the endearment, knew what it meant, but attached no meaning to its significance. It was like an action star from the old movies calling someone "sweetheart". Still, she had been remiss in not leaving a note.

She grimaced as she moved past him. "I know. I'm sorry. I should've let you know. I thought I'd be back before you woke up."

"Where have you been?" he demanded. "You've been gone for hours."

Helen thought that was an exaggeration, but she set the bags down on the kitchen table and moved to fill the kettle, plugging it in and switching it on. "I went for a quick jog then I did some shopping."

"Shopping? Faire du shopping? Could it not have waited?"

"Not if you wanted breakfast," she replied, dryly.

The kitchen door banged open and Guy walked in, still rumpled in the clothes he'd obviously slept in, and also barefoot. He started saying something in French then caught sight of her and subsided. "Oh. I see you've found her."

"It appears she was never lost. Merely," Yves glanced at the groceries she was unpacking, "buying food."

"Ah." He considered that, then grinned. "Bien."

The taller man let out a long breath. "Oui, I suppose so." He was still for a moment as if reliving an unpleasant memory then his lips quirked. "Do I have time to get dressed before breakfast?"

Helen slanted him a glance then looked away. "I think so."

When he left, it was like a void formed in the room, and Helen couldn't help the small sigh that escaped her. She had it bad. She didn't even have to look around to see where he was, she just knew, by the tingle along her skin or the prickling of her scalp. And all she had was a week. One week before he tied up the loose ends and flew back to Europe. What would he end up doing about Alexandrov? She didn't know. If anything indicated the futility of their relationship, it was that one fact. She was responsible for his personal safety, yet she knew that the job ended — firmly and irrevocably — at the shores of the country. Once he flew beyond Australia's boundaries, his well-being ceased to be her concern.

"Would you like some help?"

For a moment, she'd forgotten Guy was even there. She turned and smiled at him. He was also a good looking man, younger than Yves — perhaps around her own age — with warm brown-green eyes instead of the blue glaciers she found so compelling. Why couldn't she have fallen for Guy instead? Then the what-if questions that echoed in her mind wouldn't sound so desperate, so hollow. She ran her gaze from the top of his head, down his rumpled sleepwear, and to his bare toes that twitched self-consciously.

"I think I'll be fine," she told him warmly. "You'll have to line up for the bathroom, but why don't you go get ready while I start on breakfast?"

He nodded and left the room.

Helen decided to cook a more traditional Australian breakfast. It might not be the healthiest choice or the favourite of her two French guests, but it meant she could work on automatic and do some thinking while she prepared the meal.

With deft fingers, she liberated the sausages and bacon slices from their plastic coverings, piling them into a frying pan she set on the stove, and put aside half a dozen eggs to scramble. After switching on the oven to a low temperature, she pulled plates from one of the cupboards above the counter and rummaged for three mostly matching sets of cutlery. Her parents had never been great sticklers for the latest in interior design or fashion, which was one thing she'd loved about them. They'd both been down to earth people, who'd taught her that what was inside a person was more important than the outward trappings they wore. Idly, as she beat the eggs to a froth in a bowl with some cream, she wondered what they would think of Yves. He had the ornaments of great wealth, but he was also a strong and confident man in his own right. She had seen for herself the respect he had for Guy, and the respect he had shown her—that comment about women on the drive down notwithstanding—and she wondered what he'd be like in his natural environment.

Now that she knew that Yves was safe, one of the biggest barriers to continuing an intimate relationship with him was gone. It was like a bar of a cage disappearing. It didn't mean other bars didn't exist, but it made escape easier.

Did she want that escape? Yves still wanted her, she knew, and she still wanted him. But their affair was doomed to failure. Unless... What if he invited her back to France with him? As his bodyguard? As his mistress? Would she go?

Helen groaned as she turned the sausages and slices of bacon over in the frypan. There was nothing holding her in Australia. She had already mentally distanced herself from her business in Brisbane and was in that in-between state before she focused her energies on her move to Byron Bay. Emotionally too, there was little in Australia for her, especially with her brother Nick happily living and working in northern Italy. In fact, if she moved to France, she would be closer to Nick, and they could visit each other more often.

But... She flipped the mental coin to the other side. She was definitely counting her chickens before they hatched. It seemed like a lifetime ago that Sue told her Yves was 'France's hottest property'. And, given that fact, what were the chances that he was even interested in anything more than a temporary dalliance with some woman thousands of kilometres away? Helen didn't have to think too hard to imagine him at public events, a tall, leggy, superbly coiffed female at his side. He'd be facing the cameras, an arm snaking out to hold his companion close, his brown fingers closing possessively on the curve of her waist.

Viciously, she turned the bacon and sausages onto the plates and set them in the oven to keep warm before tackling the scrambled eggs.

The bowl of eggs and cream resembled her brains, beaten up beyond reason.

"What do you want from life, Hel?" she muttered to the warming saucepan.

Did she want safety? In which case, she was best to stay as far away from Yves as possible. Or did she want passion? In which case, she should lose herself with him again. But even if she did decide on the second option, with a body that yearned for his touch, where did that leave her in a few days' time when he was officially out of her life? There was no guarantee that Yves would want her tagging back to France with him. By the sounds of things, he had more offers of companionship than he knew what to do with.

So, what did she want? More great sex and further heartbreak? Or celibacy and a sense of empty righteousness?

When the two men entered the kitchen, Helen was composed and on the edge of a decision that she knew would have an effect on her for the rest of her life.

She set the plates on the table, each containing a hearty breakfast, and doled out the bunch of cutlery that lay on the counter. Both men smelt clean and fresh, reminding her that she still hadn't had time to freshen up after her morning jog. The table was small, and they were squashed, but it felt comfortable. Yves was not going out of his way to send seduction signals across breakfast, for which she was most grateful, and even Guy looked happy as he tucked into his food.

"Did you say you have internet access here?" Yves asked near the end of their meal.

"It's in the living room, by the desk."

"I think we may have to do some work."

Guy, his mouth full, nodded.

"Perhaps we can find out how the investigation into Alexandrov is going."

Helen could understand why Yves would want to get such a dangerous and dangling sword removed from above his head. The constant threat of violence from another person was a stressful burden. But the part of her that had become super-sensitive, seeking out layers of meaning in his every word—simply because she loved him and couldn't see a future for them both—took the sentence apart, and wondered whether he said it because he was looking forward to leaving Australia. Already, it must be more inconvenient than expected, with a rival tracking him down and two separate assaults on his person. Maybe, he might think that he'd be better off back in his familiar, European environment. It was difficult to know what he thought behind those blue and mysterious eyes of his. Yves de

Saint Nerin was a man who only showed what he wanted the other person to see. Helen only wished such a trait made him more difficult to love but, alas, it didn't.

Chapter Eleven

It was evening and Yves felt well rested. Not content, but rested. Earlier in the day, Helen had driven down into the town centre — to pay for her morning grocery bill and do some more shopping, she told him. She was quite definite about the fact that he wasn't invited, although Guy was. If he weren't such a confident man, he might have felt himself waver at that moment, but what she said made sense, even in the face of his objections.

She conceded that the last assault on them in Brisbane was not inspired by Alexandrov, but refused to budge from the position that he still lie low for the next couple of days, for the sake of his safety. To his chagrin, Guy agreed, and Yves was left to the uncharacteristic sight of watching a woman he lusted after go traipsing out the door with his assistant.

His mood didn't improve when he connected his laptop to the house internet cable — no wireless here. That was something he'd have to change for the future, he thought idly — pulling up his email and finding a reply from Delphine sitting in his inbox.

He forgot he had scratched off that impulsive email, had regretted its emptiness for an instant before the events of the day overtook him, and now back it was, with her reply. Grimly, Yves opened the email and read its contents.

My dear one,
Adrienne, Theron and the children are fine. But I think you would have already known this if you had called them yourself, non?

He should have known he couldn't put one past his dear friend. A reluctant smile tugged at his lips as he continued reading.

So I must wonder the reason for your most uninformative of emails. You do not mention what Australia is like or where you have been or even if Guy has finally succeeded in annoying you over something. That boy is unnaturally perfect, in my opinion.
Even thousands of kilometres away, as I am, my feminine intuition kicks in. Have you met someone?

Yves wondered what Delphine would think of Helen. They would like each other, he thought. Helen was perhaps a little more irrepressible, but Delphine had come from a more restrained environment in the first place. And suddenly, the thought of someone meeting his best friend didn't send shudders down his spine like it normally did. It was strange and wonderful, but he actually looked forward to introducing the women to each other, and that happy anticipation was something he had never felt before in his life.

If you have, then believe I am very happy for you. Perhaps you could consider bringing her to France, rather than keeping her secret so far away?
Whatever you decide, know that I will always be,
Your Delphine

He toyed briefly with the idea of replying, of telling Delphine that she was correct, but a niggling doubt scratched at the back of Yves' brain. Yes, he wanted to tumble Helen into bed with him once more. Yes, he wanted her to see France and meet Delphine. Yes, he was actually thinking of proposing a more permanent arrangement—with Helen Collier of the brilliant tourmaline eyes, untameable hair and calm assurance. But there were questions in the back of that steady blue gaze that he still didn't have the answers to. Why was she sad? Why was she holding herself back? Did she have any ties to this country? What, or who, exactly did he have to fight in order to get her to give all of herself to him?

When she and Guy returned, full of grocery bags and good cheer, Yves could only frown and briefly run through with his assistant what he wanted to achieve that day. With any luck, they could see to the most important issues and have tasks and orders ready by the time Europe started its working day. They worked hard for hours, only pausing for a quick lunch. Helen bustled around them. No, perhaps 'bustled' was the wrong word, Yves thought. Helen moved, she flowed, around them, quiet yet with a presence of her own. She was unobtrusive, yet all he had to do was lift his head to either see her lithe figure tending to something inside or outside the house, or breathe in the floral scent of the perfume she seemed to prefer.

She would like the place at Grenoble. He knew that viscerally. She would love wandering around the formal garden, dipping into the heated pool for a leisurely swim or watching the snow softly settle on the city while sipping a hot coffee. And he would be happy to sit there, too, content to watch her while she contemplated life, to watch the emotions flit across her expressive face.

Dinner was simple and delicious and, if it wasn't for Guy hovering around, Yves could have easily imagined a scene of domestic bliss, the rich aroma of an Italian tomato sauce with pasta wafting through the house while, through the open windows, he heard the distant sound of waves crashing onto a beach. Despite his annoyance at not accompanying Helen on her shopping trip, he was actually—surprisingly—happy to remain in the house not even venturing out to look at the ocean that he knew must be only a short walk away. In Europe, he was known as an unstoppable dynamo, always on the go, thinking, dealing, negotiating, buying. By flying halfway across the world, it was like shedding old skin, revealing a new, softer Yves. Was it the distance that had wreaked such a change in his outlook...or was it due to one person in particular?

As the sky darkened, Guy took himself off for a walk along the beach. It would have been pleasant to accompany him, but Yves preferred to stay put, nodding when Helen offered a refill of the full-bodied Chardonnay they had begun drinking during dinner, watching her as she finally ground to a halt. She had run out of things to tidy, rooms to visit, and must now sit down opposite him without the shield of movement to protect her. He knew she would not be so ill-mannered to leave him alone at the end of the day, but would be forced to keep him company.

"That was a lovely meal," he complimented, his gaze skimming her figure. Ever practical, Helen wore a pair of three-quarter pants and a loose, scooped neckline T-shirt. Every now and then, as she shifted, he saw a peek of the lavender bra she wore and had the hot urge to replace its presence with his hands. Shifting, he let his hand drift down to his trousers, hiding the semi-arousal that his imagination had fired, twirling the wine glass in his hand so she wouldn't notice how much he wanted her.

"Thank you. It's nice to cook for guests."

From the tone of her voice, he got the impression that she didn't do it very often, and his heart twinged in sympathy. He, on the other hand, had a surfeit of friends and guests, ever willing to accompany him on meals. In this way, in this little house at Byron Bay, both their needs were satisfied—hers for company and his for peace.

The silence built between them. At first, it was companionable, listening to the sounds of the encroaching night, sipping their wine then it changed. Yves wasn't sure what did it. Did his gaze linger a little longer than necessary on that eminently kissable mouth of hers, or was it when the breath caught in his throat at yet another glimpse of the flimsy bra strap from beneath her shirt.

"What do you want, Helen?" he asked softly.

She licked her lips, making them glisten in the yellow glow from the floor lamp, an invitation in and of itself.

"I, I don't understand."

She did. Of course she did. But if she wanted reassurance at this point then he was more than happy to give it to her.

"You know how I feel," he told her.

Well, that wasn't strictly true. Even Yves himself wasn't quite sure what he felt for this lethal slip of a woman. There was something about her — that potent mixture of competence and vulnerability — that intrigued him, held him, made him want to explore more of the puzzle that was Helen Collier.

"And I think I know how you feel," he added. "Thanks to you, I'm safe and more relaxed than I've felt for months."

One of her eyebrows quirked. "Are you suggesting sleeping with me out of gratitude?"

It could have been a waspish comment, but her tone was dry, as if she could clearly see the edge of humour in the situation. That was yet another thing he lov-appreciated about her.

"Until now, I feel we have been driven by circumstances outside our control. By surprise, by danger. When we sleep together again," he lowered his voice to a rumbling purr and noticed the slight tremor in her body with a stab of satisfaction, "I want no guilt involved, cherie. No gratitude. Nothing that either of us can use as an excuse."

He let the words hang in the air between them, allowing her the time to think over what he was saying—and not saying. A more inexperienced man would have charged in, trying to sway her with bluster or enticements, but Yves had not risen to his current prominence by misreading people, although he conceded that Leonid Alexandrov might have been one of his rare mistakes.

She swallowed hard, obviously thinking about his words, and he felt her indecision as something tangible.

"You're going back to France next week, aren't you?" she asked quietly.

Yves silently cursed, thinking furiously. Helen was not like the other women he dated. He knew she didn't want the photos in the glossy magazines or the expensive trinkets. In a way, being with her was a very serious business because of what he saw in her eyes. Something that he usually ran away from as quickly as his legs could carry him. So, why didn't he walk away now? Why wasn't two nights in her arms enough, when it had always been so with other women? Why did the thought of her limbs entwined around his body still have the power to consume his senses?

He knew he couldn't lie to her. And it had never ever been his policy to lie to any of his other female companions. He wouldn't start now.

"Oui. If everything goes to plan, I'll be leaving next week." Adding anything more—like the fact he had already tried to mentally reschedule the next few months without success—would sound like nothing more than a flimsy excuse.

They stared at each other across the small room, and Yves thought he could read every thought that flitted through her mind. When she was a bodyguard, she might be focused and appear impervious to everything, but relaxed, her face reflected what she thought. He saw disappointment, confusion then resoluteness. When he saw the resoluteness remain ascendant, he knew she was bowing to the inevitable. Slowly, like a trainer not wanting to startle a nervous colt, he got to his feet and walked towards her. Reaching gently for her hands, he tugged lightly, and was gratified when she, too, rose. Still holding her hands, he dipped his head and captured her lips with his. It was tender and quick, a harbinger of what he wanted to do with her, and he pulled away reluctantly.

"Tonight. I will come to your room tonight. And there will be nothing between us. Oui?"

She nodded.

* * * *

Helen sat in bed. Her knees were pulled up, and she curled her arms around her legs, in the timeworn posture of a pensive teenager. Yves' question had struck a deep chord within her.

What do you want, Helen?

At one time, even three months ago, that question would have been so easy to answer. She'd wanted a pleasant life with someone she respected who, in turn, respected her. She hadn't been after a grand passion, just support and affection from a man who didn't feel threatened by her or her profession. One month ago, all she'd wanted was time to come to terms with Pete's death and with the feeling of an opportunity gone forever. She'd wanted to start her life all over again, as she had told Ryan.

One week ago, she'd wanted to get the assignment over and done with and to use the freshly injected money in her bank account to move to Byron Bay. And now? Now, she was in love with a man so far out of her reach that she might as well hope to capture a star and keep it in a jar in the kitchen.

So, after two wonderful nights, should she keep him at arms' length? It would be painful doing such a thing, but it had the advantage that she would lessen her heartbreak in the long run. On the other hand, giving in to her fantasies meant that, at least, she'd have some memories—ones not overlaid with guilt—to remember him by.

Helen's grip on her legs tightened, and she groaned then heard a small knock on her bedroom door. Taking a deep breath, she slid off the bed and padded over to the door, opening it cautiously, as if unsure of who was on the other side. At the sight of Yves' bulk, her heart started an irregular staccato in her chest. Silently, she moved to one side and let him enter.

She expected him to sweep past her, eye the simply furnished room, and sit on the bed, beckoning her forward with one finger. The window blinds were up, letting wide beams of moonlight into the room. Every move he made was clear, bathed in the bright silvery light. And he did none of those things. Instead, he stopped just inside the door and embraced her, lifting her off the floor and kissing her passionately. Hungrily. As if thousands of miles away, the door clicked shut softly behind them. After only a moment's hesitation, her hands crept up his chest, pushing aside the rough towelling of his robe, resting for a moment against the hardness of his chest, before moving upwards to curl themselves in the silky thickness of his hair.

"Do you want this, cherie?" he whispered against her lips.

"Yes."

"Just us? No excuses, no rationalisations, nobody and nothing else interfering?"

"Just us," she answered. And she wasn't lying, not even to herself.

He moved swiftly, carrying her as if she weighed little more than a feather, and Helen—fully awake this time—had never felt so petite, so feminine in anyone's arms before. All at once, she was aware of the T-shirt and sleep pants she wore and couldn't help but cringe. She had wanted to dress in something sexy and seductive, something Yves was probably more used to from the women he bedded, but the sad truth was that she didn't have anything like that, and certainly nothing she kept at the Byron house resembled such fine lingerie.

But he didn't seem to care. She felt the firm softness of the mattress at her back, and breathed in the masculine scent of the man whose hands roamed her body then coherent thought ceased.

Yves tugged the T-shirt off her head, exposing Helen's breasts in the moonlight, their cool light touching the smooth curves and highlighting the puckered nipples, gilding them with silver. She felt the chill of the night against her flesh then the heat of a questing mouth replacing the soft fabric, suckling at her and sending sharp shocks of pleasure through her body. Helen bucked and sightlessly reached for him, frantically trying to pull the robe from his body so she could feel him press against her, flesh against flesh. She moaned in frustration at her lack of success, until Yves helped by shucking out of the confining clothing.

Helen gloried in the feel of him against her, his small nipples hard and flat against her skin as his mouth captured hers again, stilling all protest. His tongue sought hers out, probing the moist, sensitive cavern, forcing a response, until her fingers dug hard into his shoulders, feeling the movement of his muscles as he shifted position. His left hand moved to cup her bare breast, pinching the sensitive flesh until it pebbled again under his touch, and then he pushed downwards, over the side of her body and under the elastic of her pants. She gasped, and he breathed that in, relentlessly continuing his onslaught, skimming his fingernails across her triangle of damp curls as he caressed her groin with the back of his hand. He had enough time to shove the pants down while Helen kicked them off then she opened her legs, welcoming his touch.

"You are so wet, cherie," he murmured into her hair. "Aching for me, oui?"

Helen swallowed a lump in her throat. "Yes, I am," she gasped.

"As I ache for you, ma petite." But he still made no move to assuage himself, content to capture her nipples with his searing tongue and send licks of pleasure coursing through her system. She arched against him, her skin taut against her ribs, silently begging him to sweetly torture her second breast as he was doing to the first. One hand was pressed against the back of his neck, the curl of his dark hair tickling her fingers, while the other grabbed at the bedsheets, holding onto them convulsively while Yves wreaked delicious havoc on her body.

She was wet with want now, but he still teased her, grazing the junction of her thighs, and she was sure he could feel the moist heat emanating from her sex. It made her feel wanton and shameless.

When he gently parted her lips, she almost bucked off the bed completely with the intensity of the sensation, then his fingers were caressing her wetness, stroking her, and she groaned out aloud, abandoning all effort at control. She was unaware that he moved, only that he was doing wonderful, sinful things to her body and she wanted more, then she felt his mouth on her clitoris and choked out a cry.

The sensations rocking her trembling body were sensual spikes, made more intense by her recent extended bout of celibacy. Had she really denied herself this, the firm flick of a tongue against her most private of places, the brush of masculine fingers against her salty wetness? She opened her legs further, feeling the small waves of sensation start to coalesce into something larger and more uncontrollable.

"Yves," she sobbed, grabbing at him with frenzied fingers, her eyes staring wildly at the ceiling, beyond comprehension. The pleasure was building, and the need to have him inside her, thrusting into her, joining her in primitive rhythm, was insatiable.

It was as though he read her mind. The silvery beams across the ceiling disappeared, replaced by his bulk as he moved above her. There was a pause, as he removed his loose pants, and she heard the quick rip of a foil packet then she felt his legs between hers, the hard length of his penis slowing pushing into her, the delicious friction once more firing the ripples of an imminent climax. His dark eyes glittered in the night, his expression taut with the sexual tension that also gripped her. Then they were moving together, Helen working up a counterpoint to his movements, increasing the feel of him inside her as she tilted her hips. Her fingers dug into his shoulders, and she had a moment to register his skin, hot and slick, before her world shattered.

The cries she uttered seemed to come from another person. Helen was unaware of them ripping from her throat. Dimly, as if through a veil, she heard Yves' cries of release, then there was a moment of respite before he rolled over so she was on top of him, and he kissed her deeply. She felt the solid thudding of his heart beneath her torso, the frantic pounding settling down to something more sedate, and—as if it was even possible—fell in love with him a little bit more. His arms were strong and gentle around her and she felt cradled, treasured, next to his heart. It was a feeling she never thought she'd experience, more used to male partners who wanted to show off their independence in front of her. But Yves seemed content just to hold her. He landed a gentle kiss on her hair, and she melted into his embrace.

"I would like to stay with you tonight," he said softly.

"Yes."

His arms tightened at her quiet answer, then relaxed, moving her so they were both in a more comfortable position. Helen's eyes felt heavy, Yves' steady breathing acting as a lullaby, slowly sending her to sleep. He got up briefly, but was soon back, pulling her into his arms, and Helen forgot her profession, her recent grief, her dissatisfaction with her life. Warm arms enfolded her, and she fell asleep.

* * * *

The weight across her waist was unfamiliar but welcome. Helen woke to a room bathed in strong yellow light, and she grimaced as she remembered that she hadn't drawn the blinds the night before. Then she remembered what she had done the night before, and a slow heat crept along her cheekbones.

She had been shameless, there was no other way to put it. And insatiable. Oh, she couldn't believe how insatiable she'd been! She and Yves' first bout of lovemaking in the bedroom had been only the first of many, interspersed with contented naps before one of them reached again for the other. At one point, she had scrabbled in the dark herself for a pack of condoms she had bought on impulse months ago, the small box still wrapped in cellophane. It crinkled as she ripped at the covering, and she'd felt embarrassed, until Yves moved up—unabashed in his nakedness—chortling quietly while he helped her liberate the box's contents.

She moved...and groaned. There were muscles aching that she'd never even knew existed. Yves must have heard her, because his hand tightened and he pulled her closer.

"Tired, cherie?" he asked, slanting her a wicked smile.

If Yves looked dark and mysterious in the moonlight, he looked like a deity bathed in the early morning sun. The last two times they'd been together, other circumstances had intervened. But now that Helen had the luxury of drinking him in, she realised he was even more magnificent out of clothes than in them. The scrap of bedsheet covered her more than it did him, only barely concealing his hips. Helen saw the line of fine dark hair arrowing down beneath and sheet and tried not to salivate. She wanted him again. Now. Hard. Then she realised that they weren't alone in the house, and quickly closed her eyes.

"Guy," she said. She had forgotten about him during the night, but her conscious mind was back with a vengeance, reminding her of her duties and responsibilities. Of the second person she was supposed to guard.

"Mais oui. We should perhaps maintain the proprieties in front of my young and impressionable assistant."

There was laughter in his voice, but she knew without a doubt that he would indulge her in this. The man she had protected for the past week was the same one she made love to—strong, caring, and compassionate. It was enough to bring a lump to her throat.

"We should get up," she told him briskly, glancing at the clock on her bedside table. It was barely seven o'clock in the morning.

He watched her with hooded eyes and, for a moment, Helen was terrified he would disagree — loving him as she did, how could she resist him if he insisted they stay in bed? — but eventually he agreed to her suggestion, and she breathed a sigh of relief as she reached for the T-shirt that lay on the floor. With such an uncertain future in front of her, it was important that she regain a grip on the reality of the situation as quickly as possible. No matter how painful that might be.

Chapter Twelve

"This is a very nice location for a house," Yves commented, the brisk sea breeze blowing part of his words away.

He and Helen were actually on the beach below the house, but she knew what he meant. She took a deep breath, and bent over, gently stretching her hamstrings. They had already run the length of the beach until well past the centre of the town itself, and Helen had beaten him back to the wooden staircase that climbed the cliff. He was in good shape, better than she thought possible considering his sedentary profession but, despite his longer stride, he couldn't keep up with her. She was the fitter of the two which, considering her profession, was exactly as it should be.

It must have been obvious to Guy what went on the night before. When she and Yves entered the kitchen, he was already there, humming softly as he read through the local paper. He had already walked to town to buy it, he told them, his expression bland. If there was approval, or even disapproval, in his gaze,

Helen didn't see it. Yves, too, seemed completely unperturbed, helping Helen as she got a simple breakfast together, then joining her an hour later for some exercise along the beach.

"My parents bought the house not long after they got married," she explained. "That was decades ago, when Byron was little more than a sleepy little town. Dad always had big ideas to remodel the house but Nick and I liked it just the way it was."

"Nick?"

"My brother. He lives in Turin now, working as a programmer for an Italian company. We talk, but don't get to see each other too often. The last time was a couple of years ago."

Remembering where her brother was reminded her of the place Yves was returning to. She twisted and started walking up the beach. Silently, uninvited, Yves matched her steps.

This was a lovely part of the world, and Helen didn't regret her decision to move here. Although not supporting the same kind of population that Brisbane did, Byron Bay was still a lively and internationally-minded township. The place hosted music festivals, book events, and was a popular tourist destination for families from up and down the eastern seaboard.

There would be plenty to keep her occupied here, Helen told herself firmly. But she couldn't help but think of the week ahead of her as days slowly slipping between her fingers, never to be recaptured. She knew she would never forget Yves, but would he feel the same way about her? Would he even remember her when he was at some chic Paris café, sipping coffee while a beautifully dressed European woman nattered away in a multitude of languages? Helen was proud of who she was, what she was, but she had to admit that, in Yves' exclusive world, it added up to nothing more than another working girl, forced to use her wits and skills in order to make a living for herself.

"You are walking as if the hounds of hell are pursuing you, cherie."

His dark, accented voice pulled her back to the present, and she slowed her steps with a quick smile of apology. She looked down the coastline, at the ribbon of white sand, glinting in the mid-morning sun. Was this what waited for her in the future? Long, solitary walks down the beach? Hours spent mulling over options that were never available to her? She doubted she would ever find the same kind of passion with another man as she had found in Yves' arms, and that made the future look even bleaker. Before, she had been content with someone like Pete, steady, supportive and non-threatening. But now, after tasting heaven with Yves, she knew she could never settle for second-best again. Which meant she was looking at decades of a lonely life. She wanted to wail that it was all so unfair but she had brought this upon herself by agreeing to having sex with Yves in the first place. He had not forced her. She had made the decision of her own volition. And not just once. She would now have to bear its painful consequences.

He took her hand, his fingers slipping easily between her cooler ones, and she looked up at him with surprise. He couldn't know what she was thinking, yet his touch was warm and supportive, and Helen was torn in two.

Without speaking, they walked down to the edge of the water, splashing in the occasional small waves that lapped at their feet as they strolled along the beach.

If Helen wanted to save what little sanity she had, she should end it now. She knew that. Just holding Yves' hand, knowing there was no future for them together, was like a knife in her gut. After one heavenly week together, she should distance herself from him, remembering the days that were inexorably ticking by, and start to shield herself from his inevitable departure — if she wanted to save her sanity. But she couldn't think so logically, not any more. Not when her heart was involved.

Put a knife-wielding assailant screaming and running towards them right now, and Helen knew instinctively what to do. But hold the hand of the man she had fallen in love with, and she was lost.

"You are very quiet, cherie," he finally remarked in a voice that barely carried above the gentle surf.

"I'm just thinking," she replied absently.

He pulled her to a standstill, looking down into her face and searching her expression. Helen didn't know what he was after. "Sad memories, perhaps?" he prompted.

Oh no, those were yet to come. She tried to smile but knew it to be a small, sad thing.

"Work," she tried to say lightly. And both of them knew she was lying.

* * * *

The first night set the tone for the rest of their time together, a time of fantasy out of the drudgery of real life. Guy, astute and accommodating, made himself scarce, insisting that he was enjoying a time of relaxation quite rare while in Yves' employ. He was so gracious and good-humoured that Helen had no choice but to accept his explanations.

Both she and Yves woke late each morning, and the men worked in the corner of her living room while she got groceries, ran some errands and exercised. She took the opportunity to scout out some possible locations for her business while in town and had found a good potential site above a hair-dressing salon. The large, pane-glass windows along the front overlooked the ocean and let in the morning light, and there was enough space to hold small classes. In fact, the entire floor was completely bare, except for two bathrooms and a small kitchen that had already been built at the back, near the rear stairway. The place had been vacant for more than a year, and needed to be cleaned, painted, and re-floored, but Helen wasn't afraid of the work involved. The rent, considering the length of the vacancy, was reasonable, and it was near the centre of town, which meant she could walk home if she was in the mood for a stroll. The money from her current assignment was more than enough to cover the first few months' rental, leaving her time to sell her apartment in Brisbane. Yet, she still hesitated. Signing the papers meant committing herself to a life in Byron. A life without Yves. And she wasn't prepared for that quite yet. Besides, as she told the real estate agent, the property had already stood vacant for such an extended period of time. An extra two weeks wasn't going to make that much of a difference.

In the afternoons, Yves and Guy really got busy, connecting to their colleagues in Europe at the start of their day. Helen could tell from the timing that most of Yves' business interests were in Europe. The deal with Tech-88, he told her, was the first for him in the Asia-Pacific region, and he was hoping it would be the start of many.

The two men would continue through to the evening, accepting a working dinner more often than not, and only finish in time for some late-night shows. Guy would take his nightly stroll down by the beach. And Yves and Helen would retreat to her bedroom for another night of glorious sex.

Helen knew there was no other word for it. And, like a kid in a candy store, she couldn't get enough. Every stroke across his body, across his hair-roughened chest and muscular brown arms, invited more. Every kiss they exchanged, deep and drugging, demanded a repeat. Every time they came together, Helen could only think of the unutterable pleasure he was giving her, and yearn for another passionate coupling. He whispered French words in her ear, the soft syllables zipping to her brain like the highest-quality aphrodisiac and, like an addict, all she could do was wish for more.

It was a fairytale interlude and, like the tales in books she had loved as a child, Helen knew the time would inevitably come when Yves would leave. When she would be left, a ripped and broken heart in her hands, a shell of the woman condemned to greys after being shown the paradise of vivid colour. She wondered if she was strong enough to survive the inevitable heartbreak.

* * * *

"I've changed my plans," Yves announced, on the eve of their departure back to Brisbane.

Helen stilled from where she was drying and putting the dinner plates away and turned towards him. Guy, his arms in suds up to his elbows, quickly flicked the soapy water from his hands and did the same.

"We have to return to Tech-88 to sign the final papers tomorrow," he continued.

Helen nodded. "That's right," she said slowly, wondering what he was thinking. "We'll leave in the morning and get there in plenty of time for the afternoon meeting."

"Guy and I would then have to stay in Brisbane for three more days until our flight leaves for France."

Yes, she knew that, and swallowed hard, hoping he didn't see the movement. What would they do for those three days? Come back to Byron? Stay at Heritage House? Or go somewhere else? She felt torn in two. Her brain told her that the sooner Yves and Guy left, the safer they would probably be. Her heart begged her to find some reason to keep them in the country.

"But I have just been in contact with my office in Paris and with the police department in Lyons."

Yes, that would explain the quick French conversation that took place in the living-room. Yves was on the phone almost every evening, though, so she hadn't thought much of it. She wondered whether it was a premonition that a wave of goosebumps now danced up her arms. Staying quiet, she clutched the plate tightly.

"It appears," Yves said to them, after a long pause, "that Leonid Alexandrov has been apprehended."

A grin of relief split Guy's face. "Mon dieu! That's wonderful news. Fantastique!"

But there was something else. Helen saw it in the tightness around Yves' eyes, and the stubborn set to those luscious lips of his.

"Did someone get hurt?" she asked quickly.

"Non. It was an early-morning raid, and they caught him without incident."

He locked gazes with her and, for a moment, it was as though they were the only two people in the room. In the universe. There was something he was trying to tell her, but she couldn't read his expression well enough to decipher what he was trying to silently say. Finally, he broke the contact and took a deep breath.

"With this in mind, I've changed our plans. We'll be flying back to France early tomorrow evening."

Tomorrow?

Helen's head reeled and her hand closed over the dinner plate so convulsively she thought she might break it.

"But," she started to protest then ground to a halt. What did she want to say? But I don't want you to leave? But I love you? But you promised you'd stay for a few more days?

"We will still pay our agreed fee to you," Yves assured her, obviously misreading the start of her protest. "Including a bonus for the additional telephonic and internet expenses. After we sign the papers, you can take us to the airport. We should be there in plenty of time to make our flight."

"I'll call Ryan and let him know. He said he'd have someone else waiting for us at Tech-88. But what about your clothes in Heritage House?" she asked through bloodless lips. Her voice sounded faint in her ears.

Yves shrugged, a typical Gallic gesture. "I'll organise to have our things packed and shipped back to us after we leave."

Of course. As if she needed reminding of the chasm between their positions, here was one more piece of evidence showing Helen how unsuited they were together. Yves just had to snap his fingers to have people halfway around the world running to do his bidding. She could barely sign a lease contract without double and triple-thinking through the financial ramifications. Suddenly, despite the warmth in the house, she felt cold seep into her body.

She nodded at his words, not trusting herself to speak.

Yves hesitated for a second then, with a curt movement of his head, moved back to the living-room to where he'd set up his laptop, leaving Helen gripping the tea-towel much too tightly while she hoped the ground would open up and swallow her.

* * * *

Things had not gone precisely the way he'd anticipated.

Yves bit back an exhalation of frustration and tried to relax in the car. Beside him, Helen drove with a single-mindedness that verged on abnormal, her hands tight on the steering wheel, her head shifting neither left nor right. Guy wasn't saying a word either. It was like sitting in a moving tomb.

He knew she was hurt by the sudden change in his plans, but he didn't care…did he? Helen Collier might be beautiful, strong, capable, and yet achingly vulnerable, but there were other duties and tasks that awaited him on the other side of the world. Tasks that didn't include a blonde with uncontrollable hair and eyes the colour of sparkling tourmaline.

Don't forget the passion.

Merde, as if he could do that! He shifted once in the seat, despite himself. The passion. No other woman had ever come alive in his arms the way she did. She made up for her relative lack of experience with a tight body that drove him wild, an enthusiasm that seemed boundless, and the face of a wanton angel. Just the thought of her writhing in his arms was enough to make him hard, and Yves tried thinking of his house in Grenoble in order to distract him from his carnal thoughts.

It didn't help.

The spacious rooms and features that he had thought and planned over for months now seemed cold and austere in his mind. There was no sense of pride in what he had accomplished. It was, after all, too big for just one person, and he doubted his sister and her brood would be visiting any time soon. Not if an unforgiving Theron had anything to do about it.

He brooded on his brother-in-law, a man he always thought of as the eternal playboy, and how he had changed after marrying Adrienne. Did Theron, before his marriage, have the kind of conflicting thoughts that were currently plaguing Yves? Did Theron yearn to show Adrienne his family estate in the Champagne region in the same way he wanted to whisk Helen away to the glittering lights of Paris and the calm serenity of Grenoble? Could he have developed feelings for his bodyguard?

Certainly, there was something there, deep in his heart. Something special in a place he thought no woman would ever reach. But was it love or just a special variation of lust? Would it burn itself out in a matter of weeks, or did it have the potential to lead to something more permanent?

He shook his head slightly and stared out the window, as the outskirts of Brisbane flashed past. Neither Helen nor Guy were to know, but the reason he so ruthlessly cut short the trip by three days was so he could return to work. Return to work and clear the backlog of decisions and appointments that he knew waited for him as quickly as he could. For he had already convinced himself that a return trip to Australia was warranted. Not that it was the concern of anyone else, but he had to know if what he'd found with Helen Collier was just the reaction of sex with an attractive woman in unusual circumstances. Or something more. Maybe, in the interim, she would forget him, although the passionate, almost desperate, response he'd wrung from her the night before seemed to indicate otherwise. On the other hand, maybe he would forget her, finding more important things to capture his energy and focus. Somehow, he doubted it, but he still had to be sure. His reputation, even in situations of risk, was one of supreme confidence in the quality of his own decision-making. Whether it was business or personal, that remained true.

He had to be sure.

It seemed they took a fraction of the time to reach Brisbane than the time it had taken to leave it. Helen tooled the car into Tech-88's car-park with confidence. Yves could almost feel the cloak of her profession settle around her again, turning her from a lively and smiling young woman into a cool and controlled professional. As impressed as he always was by her attitude, he couldn't squash an errant feeling that he preferred Helen the person to Helen the bodyguard.

The meeting with Scott Nelson and Ian McFarlane was almost anti-climactic, the signatures only a formality to close off the current stage of negotiations. Helen was silent throughout the signing, looking impassive. Only the brighter shine of her eyes indicated there was anything other than aloof interest in the proceedings.

With a small smile, Yves took his leave of his new Australian partners and, with brief wishes that they would meet again soon, the three of them walked back to the car-park.

"You'll be wanting to go to the airport now?" Helen asked, and the control in her voice was admirable. Despite her tone, however, she looked distracted. He wondered if that was because nobody from Greenwood's security firm had met them yet. Still, in two hours' time, it wouldn't matter.

Yves nodded, and turned to the car.

He was too relaxed. Later, that's what he would tell himself as he replayed the awful events of the following minutes in his mind.

First, there was a flurry of movement. He turned, in time to see a desperate-looking youth coming straight for him, a handgun in his shaking right hand. He only had time to widen his eyes in shock, to wonder what in the world was going on, before Helen stepped in front of him.

Everything stilled to slow motion, frame by frame. His mind appeared to be working at normal speed, but his body was like a stick of clay, stuck to the floor and immovable.

Non, Helen! You cannot do this!

Guy was on the other side of the car, too far away to do anything. There was another movement off to his right, from the direction of the car-park's entrance, but Yves couldn't seem to make his eyes work the way he wanted them to. All he could do was stare at the terrible scene unfolding in front of him, while thoughts ran through his head faster than action.

She moved forward, swiftly yet calmly. Another figure approached from the side. The young man stared at him for a moment from beyond Helen's shoulder, a look of surprise and panic on his face. Then came the terrible, flat sound of a gun discharging. Helen's body, carried forward by momentum, crashed into the attacker. And the second man, not coming for him, finally snapped into focus as he threw himself into the middle of the chaos.

"Helen!" That voice, so full of fear and pain, was that him?

Yves didn't care. When time once more resumed its normal pace, and his limbs could finally move, he rushed over to the small group on the floor. There were things that didn't make sense here, but he didn't care. Careless of whether his attacker was still in possession of his weapon, he grabbed Helen and pulled her away, running a frantic gaze down her body. She was dishevelled, breathing heavily, her clothes were askew but — to Yves' eternal relief — there were no splotches of sticky, red blood anywhere on her.

Yves hand began shaking, and he didn't know whether to release her or hold onto her and never let her go. Helen, oblivious to the thoughts ricocheting through his mind, turned to the second man, visibly steadying her breathing.

"Thanks." There was such a wealth of emotion in that one word, Yves couldn't help the spike of jealousy that ripped through him. Who was this man who had stopped the attacker? Yves didn't care. He wanted to kill him as well.

"My fault. Should've been here quicker." He was an older man, moving with steady grace. He bent down and restrained the attacker by moving the young man's hands behind his back and restraining them with a plastic tie he flicked out of his pants pocket. As he stood, he flipped a phone out of a different pocket and put a call in to the police.

What the hell was going on?

Yves looked from one person to another, but the only person who met his gaze was Guy. His assistant was as stunned and confused as he was.

"Would someone care to explain exactly what's happening?" Yves demanded. He sounded angry, even to his own ears. Good. That meant nobody would notice the abject terror that had held him motionless when he'd thought Helen had been shot.

Helen pinned a tired but sincere smile on her face, clapping the older man on his shoulder. "Yves, I'd like you to meet my employer. Ryan Greenwood."

Ah.

"Under the circumstances," Yves told him dryly, "I'm very glad to meet you."

Ryan looked him up and down, lingering on Yves hand where it still held onto Helen.

He must have noticed the tremors in Yves' fingers. And perhaps more, because his gaze became speculative. "You must be Yves Nerin."

"Oui." He nodded to his assistant. "And this is Guy Aubrac."

"I'm sorry I'm late, but Nicolas here was a bit of a difficult one to track."

"Nicolas?" Yves frowned but stubbornly retained a grip on Helen. And Ryan Greenwood could make of that what he damn well pleased. "That sounds –"

"Yep. Russian. Another one of Alexandrov's little, second-rate thugs."

"But Alexandrov has been apprehended," Helen cut in. "Yves told me last night that he'd been arrested."

"Maybe," Ryan commented, "but Nicolas didn't know that. Listen, can we save all this for the police? I don't want to have to repeat myself."

A look of understanding passed between Helen and Ryan. A look Yves didn't like. It hinted at something special between the two of them. Like a thunderbolt,

Yves realised that he didn't want anything special to develop between Helen and another man. Friendship was bad enough, but anything more was unbearable. He gritted his teeth and looked away, but kept the grip on Helen, as if she was his lifeline. And he was a drowning man.

* * * *

"You've missed your flight," Helen said softly, as they exited into the night.

It had been a gruelling five hours at the local police station, explaining everything that had happened, from the initial assault at New Farm to Ryan obtaining information on the second of Alexandrov's petty criminals to the delay in getting to Helen before the young Russian did.

"I knew I was supposed to meet you at Tech-88," he told Helen apologetically, "but my source was late to our rendezvous. By the time he told me what was going on, and what Nicolas was planning, I barely had time to get there. I had to park in another street and jump a couple of fences or risk Nicolas escaping."

"You're obviously fitter that you look," she teased, but didn't try to shield the gratitude in her eyes.

The police officer who took their statements was furious that the two Frenchmen, Helen and Ryan had kept quiet about the entire episode from the start. They all knew there were more explanations they'd need to make. But, for now, they were free.

Already, night had fallen, although there was still a tinge of pale blue at the western horizon, and it was clear they were all exhausted.

"Could we invite you to Heritage House?" Yves asked Ryan. "I'm sure we could all use a good meal."

"I have one waiting for me at home," Ryan demurred. He eyed Yves with a keen gaze. "I don't think you need to worry about more attacks. For real, this time. Nicolas mightn't have got the message this morning that his employer had been arrested, but I'm sure the news would've reached everybody else by now. Have a drink for me, and I'll see you tomorrow." He paused next to Helen. "You take care."

She punched him playfully in the arm. "Of course I will." And she watched him disappear into the darkness.

The three of them were silent as they caught a taxi to the riverside residence, as if adrenaline had overloaded their systems, leaving neither the will nor the energy for conversation. The staff welcomed them in without a flicker of surprise, and an order for food was sent to the kitchen straight away.

Helen, at a loose end, unsure of what to do, walked to the large glass doors at the back of the foyer and let herself out into the back garden. She knew she should have gone for a shower, to wash the events of the last few hours from her skin, but she was too restless for such a mundane task. Someone came to stand next to her, and she closed her eyes as she breathed in Yves' distinctive cologne. It was faint and mixed with sweat, dust and an undertone of car grease, but it was still the most erotic aroma she had smelt in her life.

"As Ryan said, nobody should be bothering you any more," she remarked not knowing what else to say. Leonid Alexandrov had more important things to worry about now than getting even for a failed business proposal months before.

"Non."

It took every ounce of self-control she had, but she turned to face him. His face was dark in the shadows, and maybe that was for the best, although she couldn't help but wish for one more look into that gorgeous face of his, to stamp it into her memory for the long years ahead.

"You don't need a bodyguard any more, do you?" she asked baldly.

He shook his head. "Non."

That was her answer. There wasn't even a moment's hesitation in his voice. He didn't need her. So what was she doing still hanging around, like a forlorn puppy? Yves had made his feelings clear and, if she had any scrap of pride left, she should pack her things and leave.

She straightened her shoulders and stepped around him. "Then I'll go pack."

He caught her arm, just as he had in the car-park, where she had imagined she felt tremors against her skin. Except the thought was preposterous. It must have just been reaction on her part. Just like now, when the touch of his hand on her flesh sent spears of excitement rippling through her.

"Non."

He was making things unbearable. She wrenched her arm from his grip.

"I think it would be best for all concerned—"

"It all happened in slow-motion," he said, interrupting her. He looked at the river, the ripples like white glittering threads amongst the darkness.

His voice was quiet, as still as the rest of his body. Helen stared at him, unnerved by the lack of expression in his voice, and the profile that seemed carved from ice.

"And I couldn't move," he continued, still staring at the far shore. "It was as if my feet were stuck in cement. All I could do was watch. It was like a nightmare. Like one of the worst movies I've ever been forced to see. I wanted to..." He made an abrupt movement with his hand. "I wanted to rush. To save you." He looked down at her, and there was an unusual glitter in his eyes.

Gasping, Helen took a small step closer, her own face compressing into lines of anguish.

"Yves—"

"And it occurred to me that nothing I had was worth anything. I could not use my money to save you. To stop that crazy, young man. Not my money or my influence. In fact..." He swallowed. "It was because of my money that your life was in danger to begin with."

She couldn't stand him like this. Where was the playful, arrogant man she'd fallen so much in love with? This side of Yves had the capacity to rip her apart. She put her left hand over his clenched fist.

"That's my job, Yves," she told him softly. "That's what you paid me for."

He shook his head, slowly. "Then I was wrong. And I shall pay for such a mistake for the rest of my life." He gripped her hand. "Come with me. To France."

They were exactly the words she'd hoped for, yet Helen was shocked to hear them in the night air. "But—"

His eyes softened. "Let me show you my world. Let me worship you with my body. Helen Collier…" He took a deep breath. "Marry me."

"M-marry?"

He took a deep breath. "It seems strange that I have to thank a young thug for bringing me to my senses, but so be it. I wanted to come back to this country — that's one of the reasons I was in such a hurry to leave, so I could tidy up my affairs before heading back — but I still blinded myself to how much you meant to me. Foolishly, I tried to demean you to the status of a mistress, of fleeting enjoyment. Until that moment in the car park, when I wanted to give my life for yours, and accepted that I had fallen too deeply in love with you to further delude myself." One corner of his mouth curved upwards in a crooked smile. "If you'll have me, that is."

Helen laughed, but it came out as a half-sob. With her left hand captured so effectively, all she could do was bang on his chest with her right fist. "Oh, you devil. I was prepared to walk away, and since this afternoon, you've been thinking of proposing."

He brought both hands against his chest as he chuckled. "Do you love me?"

"God help me," she said, struggling, "but I do."

"Enough to put up with me for the rest of your life?"

She stopped and looked up at him in wonder. "You're serious, aren't you?"

"Do you doubt it?" he asked, a touch of his usual hauteur colouring his tone.

"No," she smiled, "no I don't."

"Then after we seal this latest bargain, I suggest we go in and share our good news with Guy."

But it took a long time before Guy found out. And they both looked tousled as they imparted it.

Tousled. And smiling.

About the Author

I am a child of the global South. In the past, I have run my own IT consultancy business, bookshop, gym, swimming pool business and martial arts school.

So far in my life, I have been a corporate trainer, lecturer, satirist, martial arts instructor, project manager, political essayist, small business owner and am now proud to call myself a fiction writer. Although I love romance, I have to admit my first love is science-fiction and the opportunity to combine both genres was irresistible! I do hope you enjoy reading my stories.

Together with my husband, we have lived and worked in Europe, Asia, Australia and North America. We adore our two children and tolerate as necessary evils our two grumpy, fur-shedding cats.

KS Augustin loves to hear from readers. You can find her contact information, website details and author profile page at http://www.total-e-bound.com.

Total-E-Bound Publishing

www.total-e-bound.com

Take a look at our exciting range of literagasmic™
erotic romance titles and discover pure quality
at Total-E-Bound.